"An-ying? It's Joey."

My heart started pounding. I was glad Joey had called, but I was too worried about Ben to want to talk, and my mother was right around the corner. I took the phone into the hall closet.

"Hi," I said.

"I'm calling from work, so I can't stay on long. I just wanted to know if we can get together on Friday."

"I'm not sure. Can I let you know?"

"Waiting to see if something better comes along, huh?" He said it jokingly, but I could tell he was hurt.

"No, it's not that, I promise. I really want to see you. It's just that my parents are kind of old-fashioned. They don't think I should date. Especially guys who aren't Chinese."

"Hmm. I could disguise myself. Plastic surgery is an option."

I laughed. "Maybe it would be easier if I just met you somewhere."

"Great. Where and when?"

I hesitated again. I wanted to see Joey, but I knew I had to look for Ben. I wouldn't have any fun until I found him.

"An-ying?" Joey said when I didn't answer.

"My parents aren't the only problem," I said quietly. "It's my brother. He . . . he's missing, and it's my fault, and I have to find him."

Books in the REAL LIFE Series

OBSESSED
CALL ME CATHY

Available from ARCHWAY Paperbacks

For orders other than by individual consumers, Archway Books grants a discount on the purchase of **10 or more** copies of single titles for special markets or premium use. For further details, please write to the Vice-President of Special Markets, Pocket Books, 1230 Avenue of the Americas, New York, NY 10020.

For information on how individual consumers can place orders, please write to Mail Order Department, Paramount Publishing, 200 Old Tappan Road, Old Tappan, NJ 07675.

Call Me Cathy

Margaret Meacham

AN ARCHWAY PAPERBACK
Published by POCKET BOOKS
New York London Toronto Sydney Tokyo Singapore

This book is a work of fiction. Although suggested in part by certain actual events, persons and circumstances, *Real Life: Call Me Cathy* is not a factual account. Numerous incidents, details and other plot devices have been created for dramatic effect. Names, characters and places in this story are fictitious or are used in a fictitious manner. Any similarity to real persons, living or dead, is not intended.

AN ARCHWAY PAPERBACK *Original*

An Archway Paperback published by
POCKET BOOKS, a division of Simon & Schuster Inc.
1230 Avenue of the Americas, New York, NY 10020

ISBN: 0-671-87272-9

First Archway Paperback printing January 1995

10 9 8 7 6 5 4 3 2 1

Cover photo by Franco Accornero

Printed in the U.S.A.

IL 7 +

It Happened to Me . . .
It Could Happen to You.

REAL LIFE books are inspired by the lives of real people who want to share their stories with you. The books re-create important events that offered these teens many choices, many chances, and many changes. Although the actual names, places, and incidents are fictional, the characters in these books have lives just like yours, feelings just like yours, and stories that could be yours!

To Poki Yung,
with gratitude for your insight
and inspiration

Is it possible for one person to be two people? You may think it's not, but I know it is. I've been two people for a while now. When I'm with my friends, I'm an American who happened to be born in China. But to my parents, I'm a Chinese girl who just happens to live in America.

This was okay when I was a little girl, when we first came over to New York seven years ago, when I was ten. But now it's not okay. I don't want to be two different people anymore. I've tried to explain to my parents that I need to be with my friends, that I'm getting older and need more freedom. But my parents don't understand. They still treat me like a little girl, even though I'm a senior in high school. My mother says, "Chinese girls do not need freedom. They need to work hard, to have good manners. They must do their duty for the family and be obedient. If you do these things, you will have a good life."

I tried to explain it to her another way. My mother has this way of explaining things by telling stories. Sometimes it drives me up the wall. But I thought maybe if I tried it her way, she'd understand. So I said, "If a fish decides to leave the sea and go live in a tree like a bird, the fish would have to learn some of a bird's ways. It would have to learn to breathe air instead of water. It would have to learn to fly instead of swim. If it didn't learn these things, that fish wouldn't survive. It's the same with Chinese who move to America. You have to learn American ways. You can't go on pretending you're still in China."

But my mother still didn't understand. She said, "I don't care what you say about fish and birds, An-ying. We are *Chinese.* We will always *be* Chinese, no matter where we live. We could go live on the moon, but we would still be Chinese. And Chinese girls do not go out at night. Chinese girls come straight home after school. Chinese girls do not talk back to their parents."

So I go on trying to be a fish who lives in the trees, but I know things have to change. I know that if my parents don't let me learn how to fly and how to breathe air, I will suffocate.

I guess that's why on Tuesday, when my two best friends, Suni Tabor and Melissa Restivo, said they were going shopping on the way home from school, I decided to go with them. I knew my mother would be waiting, furious that I had not come home exactly at four-thirty the way I'm supposed to, but that didn't stop me.

"You've got to see these great earrings," Melissa said. "I really want them, but I don't know if I should blow every cent I've got on them. You've got to help me decide." Melissa was talking to Suni, assuming, I knew, that I wouldn't be able to go with them.

"I'll come too," I said.

Melissa grabbed my arm. "Really? I mean, they'll let you?"

"Who cares? I'm going anyway. I'm sick of being a prisoner in my own house."

Melissa made a fist and punched the air. "Yes! That's the spirit. You've got to stand up to them."

But Suni looked at me. "Are you sure, An-ying?"

I nodded. "I'm sure."

As we went into the Elle Boutique I forgot about my mother and how mad she would be. It felt so good just to be with my friends, doing something most teenagers get to do all the time. Inside the store Melissa pointed to the earrings she wanted. They were dangly silver teardrops with a black stone set in them. "Would you like me to take them out for you?" asked the girl behind the counter.

"Aren't they fantastic?" Melissa said, holding them up to her ears and studying them in the mirror. "I really want them." Melissa took off her wire-rim glasses, but without them she had to squint to see her reflection. She is so nearsighted and almost never without her glasses, although she says she hates them.

She's small, or petite I guess you'd say, and has shoulder-length strawberry blond hair. Most of the time Melissa is kind of a sloppy dresser, and pretty disorganized. She almost always wears oversize sweaters and jeans and hiking boots. She usually doesn't get too excited about clothes or jewelry, but occasionally she falls in love with something, like these earrings.

"They'll be going on sale next week," said the girl. "If you're sure you want them, I could hold them for you, and you could get them at the sale price—twenty percent off."

"That'd be great," Melissa said. "I definitely want them. Definitely."

"Okay, then, if you'll just give me your name . . ."

While Melissa made arrangements for the earrings, Suni and I looked around the boutique. There were some great hats, shaped like baseball caps but in paisley and flowered prints. I tried one on, and Suni said, "That looks great on you. You should get it."

I looked in the mirror. It did look good. "Maybe when it goes on sale," I said, although I knew I wouldn't be able to afford it then, either. My parents won't let me get a job. They won't even let me baby-sit, something most of my friends have been doing for years. I do help my mother with her sewing business, but she hardly pays me anything. I know she can't afford to pay me much, and that it's my duty to the family to help out financially, but I don't see why they won't let me have a real part-time job the way most of my friends do.

I studied the hat. "Actually, this would be easy to

make. I could do it for almost nothing," I said. Lately I'm making a lot of my own clothes, or finding things in secondhand clothing stores and fixing them up a bit. I've put together some cool outfits from bits and pieces. Up until last year I was a pretty conservative dresser, just wearing what my mother sewed for me or buying whatever was on sale. But once I realized I could create my own clothes, with a style all my own, I began to dress differently. And a few weeks ago I got a new haircut, really short for me. I always had hair down to the middle of my back, and now it's chin length. I love it, and my friends say it suits me. I went into the salon to get a trim—just an inch cut off the bottom. But Rudy, the hairdresser, told me my hair had great body and that I'd look better with a short cut. I'd always thought my hair was coarse, but he said it was bouncy. Then he showed me a picture of a short cut and said it would bring out my delicate features. So instead of getting an inch cut off, I lost about seven.

I hadn't planned on making such a drastic change. I guess I did it partly because while I was waiting for my turn in the shop, I saw all the customers coming and going, getting all kinds of stuff done to their hair—perms, highlights, you name it. It intrigued me. I thought how neat it would be to make a big change in myself, present a whole new person to the world. And I'm really glad I did it. Of course, my parents hate it. When my mother first saw it, she asked me if the woman who cut it had been drunk. My parents also hate the clothes I wear now. My mother says I dress like a peasant. She can't understand why I want to wear "other people's trash," as she calls the things I buy at secondhand shops.

Outside the boutique, Melissa said, "Let's stop at the diner. I'm starved."

I looked at my watch. I knew my mother would already be mad, but I didn't care. Maybe it was my new haircut, I don't know, but I was ready to make some changes in my life.

"What can she say about stopping for a snack?" Melissa added. Even though Melissa is really small and not at all fat, she's always hungry, and she eats as much as a football player. No one can figure out where she puts it all.

"You know my mother. She'll think of something to say," I answered. "'Made with food that is impure. Too many germs.'"

As Suni and Melissa both knew all too well, I wasn't allowed to go to Pizzatown because my mother felt it was unclean. I wasn't allowed to eat at Burger Palace —"that food will poison you, make you swell up like a rotten cow." But today I thought, I don't care. I just don't care. I want to be with my friends. I'll pay the price when I get home, but I'll worry about that later. "Let's go," I said.

As we slid into a booth at the Galaxy Diner, Suni said, "Jason said he comes here a lot. Maybe he'll show up." She has a major crush on a guy in her chemistry class named Jason Thorndike, who is, I have to admit, pretty cute.

"You mean he actually talked to you about something besides when he could borrow your chem notes? This is a real breakthrough," I said.

"Well, he wasn't exactly talking to me when he said it. He was talking to Peter Freidberg." Suni frowned. "But actually we've had several meaningful conversations lately. Yesterday, for instance, he sneezed and I said, 'God bless you,' and he said, 'Thank you.' And the day before that he asked me if I could lend him a pencil."

"Hmmm. Progress," said Melissa.

Suni nodded, all smiles. "I'm hoping he'll be at Michael's party on Friday. Michael's a friend of his, so maybe." She tucked her black hair behind her ear and moved her spoon to one side as the waiter set a cup of hot chocolate in front of her. Suni has long black hair, like mine was. She's half Chinese. Her mother came to this country when she was in her twenties and married Suni's father, a big blond American man. Her parents aren't at all like mine, even though her mother is Chinese. My parents don't approve of Suni's parents because they're a mixed couple.

"You're going to Michael's party, aren't you?" Suni asked. I knew this was meant for Melissa, not for me. They both knew that my parents wouldn't let me go to a party given by a boy they didn't know, especially a Caucasian boy.

"Are you kidding? I wouldn't miss it for anything. Do you remember the party he had last year? It was the best."

I remembered it, even though I didn't go. I remembered that Melissa and Suni hardly talked about anything else for days before and after.

Melissa looked at me. "Can't you tell them you're spending the night at my house? Just don't mention the party."

"I tried that in tenth grade, remember? When my mother found out I went to a party at a boy's house, she almost had me locked up."

"But they let you go to Martha's last week. Why not Michael's?"

I sipped my hot chocolate and said, "Well, for one thing, I told my mother it was just a bunch of girls getting together to study." I sighed. It was hard to explain, even to Suni and Melissa, who knew all about my parents.

"My father has this thing about Caucasian boys," I went on. "Remember when Philip Dyson and I were assigned to work together on that science project? Philip came to my house to work with me, and my father went nuts. He practically threw him out of the house."

I didn't even want to tell them about the time, soon after we had come to New York, that I was walking with my father in Chinatown. We had seen a young couple, a Chinese girl and a Caucasian boy, holding hands. My father nodded at them and told me, in Chinese of course, because he refuses to learn English, "If that were my daughter, she would be at home where she belongs, not holding hands with him, like a cheap prostitute." My father hasn't changed at all in the past ten years.

"Believe me," I told Suni and Melissa, "it's hopeless."

And then I saw my younger brother, Lee, outside, looking in the window of the diner. I knew my mother had sent him. She's done this before, whenever I'm the tiniest bit late getting home from school.

And suddenly I was so mad that I wanted to jump up from the table and rush home to scream at my mother. I wanted to demand that she tell me why it is that Lee, who's only eleven, is allowed to go out with his friends, to the mall or for pizza, when I'm not allowed to do anything. I wanted to ask why she doesn't worry about my older brother, Ben, who is nineteen and sometimes stays out till dawn, hanging with a bunch of creepy-looking weirdos. Ben, who lost the last job he had because he was always showing up late for work, and who never smiles anymore, never jokes and laughs the way he used to. Why do they only worry about me, when I'm the one who gets straight A's, who hardly ever disobeys, who never gets in trouble at school?

Of course I knew the answer to this. It's because I'm a girl, and Ben and Lee are boys, and in China, boys are allowed to have freedom and girls aren't. But this isn't China, I wanted to scream at them. This is America, and in America girls don't have to stay trapped in their homes cooking and sewing and waiting on men!

"God, there he is," I said, putting down my head, hoping Lee hadn't seen me.

"Who, Jason?" Suni said quickly, turning to look at

the door of the diner. "Oh," she groaned as she caught sight of Lee coming toward us. "Jeez, can't they leave you alone for ten minutes?"

"Tell me about it. But I'm not going home. I'm staying here until we're finished."

In a minute Lee was standing by our booth, looking at me. "Ma wants you," he said, and I could tell he was trying not to embarrass me by telling the whole truth—that she was having a fit because I hadn't come home on time.

"Tell her I'll be a little late," I said. "Just tell her I'll be late."

"But—"

"Never mind. Just tell her," I said, holding up my hand and fixing him with a look that told him I didn't want to hear it. Finally he shrugged and left.

Melissa looked at me and said, "Wow, I'm impressed. You really are standing up to them."

"Yeah, but what are they going to do when you get home?" asked Suni.

"My mother's probably hysterical, ready to call the police right now, but I've had it. I can't live like this anymore." I shrugged.

"They've got to understand that you're not a ten-year-old," said Suni.

"We'll start the An-ying liberation movement. We'll picket your house with posters that say 'Free An-ying,'" said Melissa.

It was funny then, but I knew that soon I would have to go home and face my mother. We finished our hot chocolate and Melissa paid, knowing that I never have any money since my parents won't let me work.

On the corner where we split up Suni took my hand and squeezed it. "Would it help if I come home with you?" she asked. "Maybe if I'm there, your mother won't go crazy." She knew my mother would never cause a scene when there was a guest in the house.

I shook my head. "Thanks, but that would only make it worse when you leave."

"Oh . . . well, call me later," she said. "That is, if you're still alive." I watched her for a minute as she headed toward her home. Such a good friend. As I walked toward my house I thought how lucky I was to have friends like Suni and Melissa.

When I turned into our front walk, I saw the curtains move, and I knew that my mother had been watching for me. The anger I had felt earlier in the diner returned, and I thought, I'm glad that Lee found me, because now I won't have to make up a lie about where I've been. I hate lying to them, and I know it's wrong, but what choice do they leave me?

My mother was no longer at the window when I came in but in the kitchen, where she usually is when I come home from school. Only instead of facing the hallway as she usually does when she works at the butcher's block, her back was to the door, telling me that she was mad. I could smell the oil from my mother's wok and the sharp odor of ginger. I watched her for a moment through the door that led from the hall to the kitchen, and I knew by her movements that she was rolling out dough for wonton. She didn't stop or turn to look at me, though, so I went on into the living room, where Lee was sprawled in front of the television, his feet propped on the coffee table.

"Did you tell her where I was?" I asked.

He nodded, eyes still on the TV. "She made me."

"What'd she say? Is she mad?" I asked.

He nodded again. "She's not a happy camper."

I threw my backpack on the couch. "I'm seventeen years old. Why should she care if I'm half an hour late coming home?"

He shrugged. "You know Ma." He looked at his watch. "Actually, you're sixty-seven minutes late."

My mother came to the door of the living room and stood looking at me, her eyes black slits and her lips compressed into a thin, straight line that was neither a smile nor a frown. Her face was blank, like a plain sheet of paper, saying nothing, revealing nothing, though I was sure she had lots to say. "Well?" she asked, speaking in Chinese.

"Well what?" I said, speaking in English. My mother's English isn't that good, but at least she's made an effort to learn it, which is more than I can say for my father.

"You are late. Over an hour late, and you have nothing to say about it? You keep me standing at the window, watching for you, wondering if you've been struck dead in the street, and you don't even apologize? I got so worried I left the vegetables on the stove and now dinner's half ruined. That's well what."

"No one asked you to watch and wait for me, Mother."

"You know you're supposed to be home at four-thirty, before dark. Now it's almost six o'clock. Dark for an hour. Dangerous. And you know it's not proper for a girl to be out on the street after dark, running around like a cheap floozy. You know this."

"We stopped off at the diner. Melissa and Suni go there almost every day. There's nothing wrong with it. Why shouldn't I?"

My mother pointed to a pile of sewing she had left for me in the hall. "You are neglecting your work."

"I sewed for three hours yesterday and two the day before. I have to do something besides sew and study."

Once again my mother turned her back on me, and even though she said nothing more right then, I knew this was not the last I'd hear of what I'd done. She would tell my father about it, and between them they would come up with some plan, some way of keeping me away from my friends, a way of keeping me from being myself.

That night after dinner I began to help my mother clear the table as usual, but my father held up his hand. "An-ying, please sit down. I want to talk to you."

My mother took the dishes out to the kitchen and began to wash them. Lee had gone downstairs to his room, and Ben was out, so it was just my father and me. Uh-oh, I thought. She's called in the big guns. I knew that my mother had told my father I got home late. My mother didn't always tell my father things. Sometimes she would say, "Your father would be displeased if he knew. I will not tell him this time." But whenever she thought I was getting out of control, she'd talk to him, and then he would talk to me. Sort of a good cop–bad cop routine.

"So you disobeyed your mother and were late coming home today?"

"I wanted to be with my friends, Dad," I said.

"Speak in Chinese, please," he said. My father never speaks English, and most of the time he insists that we speak Chinese as well. He says it's out of respect for our native language, but I know it's because he doesn't speak English very well and doesn't want to bother to learn. He went on, "You are with your friends all day in school. After school, you should be here at home. Your mother also tells me you have been disrespectful lately."

In Chinese I said, "I'm seventeen, Dad. I'm not a little girl anymore. I've got to be able to live my own life. Next year I'll be in college, probably I won't even be living here, and that's less than a year away."

"Who says you won't be living here? Where else would you live?"

"If I get the scholarship to Wharton, and Ms. Brady says she thinks I've got a great shot, then I'll be living there, in Philadelphia, in the dorm."

My father said nothing for a few minutes. He stared across the room at the opposite wall, his eyes fixed on the painting of the Yin River that hangs there, as if he were reading a message in it. After a while he nodded toward the painting. "You see that? The River Yin. My mother painted it. That was the view from our house when I was a small boy."

"Yes, I know, Dad," I said.

"Four generations of my family lived in that house. We all lived together, as families should."

"I know, Dad, but things don't always work out that way."

"This is true. They didn't work out that way for us. When I was twelve, my father and mother moved to Hong Kong. The jobs were better there, and we had more money, but I always missed that house. It was a mistake, I think, that move. In China a daughter lives with her family until she marries. To do otherwise would be shameful, an insult to your father and mother, and to your ancestors."

"But Dad, this is America. Not China. In America if a daughter wins a scholarship to a good college, her parents are proud. Only fools would turn it down."

"Well, perhaps I am a fool, but I think there are plenty of good colleges right here in New York. You can still go to college, but you can continue to live here, where you belong. Until you marry, of course. That way, everyone will be happy."

Before I could speak, he went on. "And you are to be home at four-thirty, no later. Do you understand?"

I said nothing. He waited for me to answer. When I didn't, he said, "I asked if you understand?"

"No," I said. "No, I don't understand. And I don't think you understand. Maybe in China girls live at home until they marry. Maybe in China they never get to go out and have any fun with their friends, but this is America. Land of the free, remember? That includes women."

I had never spoken to my father like that before, and I think I was almost as surprised as he was. But I was tired of never saying what I felt. Tired of being treated like a ten-year-old. I had to make my parents understand.

My father spoke in a low, controlled voice, but I knew he was furious. "We may not be in China, but we are still Chinese. We will never be like the *low faan.*" That's what he calls Americans. It means barbarians. "You will obey your parents and be home at four-thirty every day," he went on. "If not, you will be punished. Now I have work to do. Would you be so kind as to bring me some tea and a plate of biscuits?" My father opened his book and began to read.

I was so angry I wanted to grab his book and throw it at the picture of the River Yin, but I knew that would only get me into worse trouble. There was no point in trying to talk to him anymore. I stood up and went to the kitchen to get him his tea.

As I made the tea I thought about what he had said, and I realized he had no idea how I felt. Why did he move here, I wondered, if he hates American ways? It was hopeless to change him or to make him understand me. But I made up my mind. If I won the scholarship to Wharton, there was no way I was going to turn it down.

There were two reasons I was determined to go. For one thing, Wharton has a great reputation as a business school, and I knew I would get the education I needed there. With that education I would be halfway to fulfilling my dream, the dream that had been growing and taking shape inside me for a long while. In my dream, I imagine myself as the owner of my own boutique, selling beautiful fashionable clothing, some of which I designed myself. My store is unique because I have a talent for helping the women who shop there find their own style. My dream is so real to me that I can see the colors and lines of the clothes, the way they hang on the mannequins in my shop windows. I can feel the fabrics as I place them on display, and I can hear the voices of the women who come to me, grateful for my help. It is this dream that drives me, that keeps me getting A's, that gets me through the long, boring hours when I help my mother with the sewing. I haven't told anyone about my dream, not even Suni and Melissa. I kept it inside me, always there, like a treasure that I can take out and look at anytime I want.

But I had another reason for wanting the scholarship. I knew that was the only way I would be free to live my own life. As long as I stayed with my parents, I never could. And so, as I fixed my father his tea and prepared his plate of biscuits like a dutiful Chinese daughter, I resolved that I would accept the scholarship no matter what my parents said. Somehow they'd have to get over it.

That's when I thought of Aunt Su-lin. If there was one person who could reach my parents, it was my aunt. Aunt Su-lin is married to my father's brother. They came to this country five years before my parents. My uncle bought a Chinese grocery, where my father now works. They were the ones who convinced my parents to come to America.

Because Aunt Su-lin has no daughters of her own,

she looks at me almost as if I were her own daughter. When I was younger, soon after we had arrived in this country, both my parents had to work all day long. My father worked in my uncle's grocery store, my mother in a factory. Sometimes in order to help my mother Aunt Su-lin would take me to stay at her house for a night or two. I loved it because Aunt Su would treat me to all kinds of things. She took me to see my first movie and bought me my first ice-cream sundae. I grew close to Aunt Su, and we're still close. I remember the first time Melissa invited me to spend the night at her house. My parents weren't going to let me go because Melissa's not Chinese, but Aunt Su-lin convinced them they should let me. And Aunt Su loves the clothes I make, even the ones from secondhand stores that my mother hates. She says I have a very distinctive style, and that I'm truly talented. I made her an outfit for her birthday, and she loved it.

My mother sometimes gets mad at Aunt Su-lin, because she thinks she interferes too much in my life. She says, "Su-lin talks like a parrot and laughs like a hyena." She does talk a lot and has this funny laugh, but she can be pretty persuasive, and my mother listens to her more than she lets on. Maybe if I told Aunt Su-lin about my dream and explained to her why I wanted to go to Wharton, she would be able to convince my parents to let me accept the scholarship.

I decided it was worth a try, so after I had served my father his tea, I went to the phone and dialed my aunt's number.

Her cheerful voice made me feel good. "An-ying. How are you, sweetie? I haven't seen you in ages. Your mother got you sewing like crazy?"

"Yes, and I've been busy with schoolwork."

"Of course you have. With the grades you get, you must have to study all the time. Such a good student. So, what can I do for you? You need me for something, or you just calling to say hi?"

"Well, actually, Aunt Su, I need some advice. Maybe I could stop by after school sometime."

"Advice? You come to the right person. Advice I got plenty of. Maybe not good advice, but plenty of it." My aunt laughed, which made me laugh too. Aunt Su loves to give advice.

"Sometimes just talking to you helps me figure things out," I told her.

"I know what you mean, sweetie. Everyone needs someone to talk to. Tell you what. Why don't you come for dinner next Saturday? Give us a chance to catch up. Then we can talk all you want. Sound good?"

"Sounds great, Aunt Su. I'll see you then."

"All right, love. And you tell your mama not to work you so hard. A girl's got to have some fun sometimes."

We hung up, and I felt much better. Aunt Su wouldn't let my parents turn down a great opportunity like Wharton. But first I had to win the scholarship, so I went to my room to study.

I was halfway through my calculus homework when I heard the key in the lock, and I knew that Ben had come home. It was nine-thirty, which was actually pretty early for him these days. I would like to ask him where he's been and what he's been doing, but my father tells me it's not my place to question him. My mother says, "He's a man, you are a girl."

Anyway, I was glad Ben was home. Once Ben and I were very close, but lately it seemed that he was always out, and when he was home, he stayed in his room with the door closed. I was worried about Ben, and I thought my parents actually were too, even though they didn't seem to know what to do. Last summer after he graduated from high school, he got a job with a construction crew. He was planning to work for a year and save some money, and then go to night school. Then things began to change. He started spending more and more time down in Chinatown, hanging out with a weird-looking crowd of druggies and other lowlifes. He started coming home later and later at night. At first he was able to make it to work all right, but then he missed more and more time, until finally his boss got fed up and fired him. Ben had been out of work almost two months, and although he told our parents he was looking for a new job, it didn't seem to me that he was looking very hard.

I heard him thumping down the stairs to his room in the basement, and I called to him. He stopped and came back up, leaning against the doorjamb of my room. He was wearing a new leather jacket, obviously expensive, and I wondered where he had gotten the money for it.

"So. Calculus, huh?" he said.

I nodded. "Test tomorrow."

"You study too hard, little sister. You need to have some fun."

"I'll never have any fun as long as I live here. That's why I study. So I can get a scholarship and move away."

Ben came in my room and flopped down on the bed, lying back, his head propped up on his hand, his long hair brushing the top of my pillow.

"A scholarship? Big dreams, huh?"

"My adviser, Ms. Brady, says she's sure I'll get one."

"Yeah? Well, don't believe everything they tell you. They make it sound like it's so easy. Get an education, get a job, get rich." He gave a short laugh. "It's all so simple, isn't it? Let me tell you something. That's not the way it works in the real world."

I put down my pencil and swung my chair around to face him. "Do you remember when we first moved here, how excited Dad was? How he took us all over New York, showed us the Statue of Liberty, and took us to a baseball game? He used to talk about America as if it were the greatest place in the world."

Ben nodded. "He used to say we were going to America to find gold. Hmm. Some gold."

"But the grocery store is doing okay, isn't it?"

He shrugged. "Okay, but who wants to slave their life away selling rice and fish? He'll never get rich that way. There's only one way to get rich around here."

"You mean go to college and get a decent job?" I

said, hoping maybe he'd changed his mind about going on in school.

But he laughed and looked up at the ceiling. "Maybe for you, little sister, but not for me. That would take too long. There are better, quicker ways."

"Like what? What do you mean?

"Never mind. You just keep on working for that scholarship. Who knows? Maybe you'll get it."

I didn't like what Ben was saying about quick ways to make money. Maybe I was only a high school kid, but I knew most of the quick ways of making money were illegal. And he always had money lately, even though he wasn't working. He also got a lot of calls from people I never heard of. He was always very secretive about these calls, making sure no one could hear what he was saying.

"Oh, by the way, I've got something for you," Ben said, sitting up. He opened the sports bag he always carried and pulled out a brand-new Sony Walkman, the most expensive model, with every special feature on it—the kind I'd been dying for ever since my old cheap model broke.

"Ben, I can't take this."

"What do you mean, you can't take it? Since when can't you take a present from your brother?"

"But . . . it's too expensive. How can you afford it?"

"Don't worry about that. Just listen to it, and enjoy it." He looked at his watch. "Almost ten. I've got to call Freddie. He's got a line on a job for me." He was up off the bed and halfway out the door before I could say anything more. "Later, little sister. Don't work too hard."

When he was gone, I picked up the Walkman, put in a tape, and listened. The sound was great, much better than my old one. But somehow instead of making me happy, as Ben wanted, the gift made me sad. I couldn't explain it, but I knew that something about it wasn't right. Ben was out of work. Where was he getting his money?

3

For the next few days I made sure to be home on time after school and worked hard on my sewing, trying to help my mother as much as I could. I was waiting for the right moment to bring up Friday night. I decided I was going to Michael's party. I knew I couldn't tell my parents the truth, so I'd tell them I would be home late Friday night.

Thursday morning at breakfast my mother seemed in a pretty good mood, so I said, "By, the way, Ma, I'll be late coming home on Friday. I'm going to Suni's. It's her birthday, and her family's having a birthday dinner for her. I'll be home around eleven."

"Eleven? Why so late?"

"It's not that late. Melissa's parents will give me a

ride home. Or maybe I should just spend the night there?"

Ma said nothing for a minute, and I thought she was just about to say okay, but then the news came on the radio and we heard: "The violence that erupted last night in a West Side convenience store ended in the deaths of two teenagers. . . ." Ma shook her head, pointing to the radio. "You see. Listen to that. It's not safe. It's dangerous out there, people getting shot all the time, racial violence, gangs. You see why I worry?"

I wanted to smash the radio right then, but instead I took a deep breath and tried to be cool. I said, "Look, Ma. I know it worries you when I'm out, but just because there are some crazies out there is no reason to stay home all the time. I have to have a life besides school work and sewing."

"I just want you to stay away from the danger and prejudice."

"I won't be anywhere dangerous, Ma."

"Be home by eleven," she said. She turned back to the sink, saying nothing more, and I knew that was the last I would get out of her for now. It was enough.

I finished my breakfast, grabbed my backpack, gave my mother a quick kiss, and went out the door. Out on the street I looked back at the house and saw Ma watching me from the window next to the front door. I knew she worried about me, about all of us, just like all mothers worry. And I knew how hard it had been on her, leaving China and all of her family. I remember that when we left, my father was excited, but my mother cried. Once we got here and things hadn't gone the way my parents had hoped, though, it was my mother who was cheerful and tried to raise everyone's spirits.

I thought back to our first year in America, when I was in the fifth grade. For the first month we stayed with my aunt and uncle, and everything had been so new and exciting. We were like starry-eyed children, even my parents, believing that we were really going to make it in what we thought was the land of opportunity.

But it hadn't taken long for reality to set in. My parents found out that jobs were really hard to get, especially since neither of them spoke English. My uncle couldn't afford to pay my father more than a few dollars an hour to work in his grocery store back then, but Dad had to take the job, working long hours for less pay than he had made back in Hong Kong. My mother found work in a sewing factory, but she had to leave the house at six in the morning, and most nights she didn't get back home until seven or eight. Even though they were both working, they still weren't making that much, so the only apartment we could afford was tiny. It had just one bedroom, which my parents shared with my brothers. I had to sleep in the living room. Since Ben and I were in school, there was no one to watch Lee, who was only four. My mother had to take him with her to the factory. All day he had to sit or sleep right beside her. If he caused any trouble, my mother knew she wouldn't be able to bring him, and she would have to quit her job.

I also remember sitting in school the first few weeks

of fifth grade and not understanding anything the teacher said. I tried to do my homework, but half the time I didn't even know what the assignment was. I had to use my English/Chinese dictionary to look up every word. Just reading one paragraph took forever. But I was determined to learn English and to do well in school. It was so important to me, partly because I wanted to prove that I could do it, but also because I knew what a sacrifice my parents were making so that my brothers and I would be able to get a good education. One of the main reasons they had decided to come to this country was us, so that we could be educated here. I thought of my mother working all day in that factory, with my little brother curled up beside her, and I knew I had to get good grades.

Every day I came home and went right to work, trying to teach myself English. The worst thing was that there was no one to help me. My parents hardly spoke any English at all, and there was no one else. Gradually my English got better, and halfway through the year I was doing all right. My grades in math were good, but subjects that required a lot of reading were still hard. I remember that about that time I had to take an English-as-a-second-language test. They sent the results home, and I opened the envelope before my parents got there. When I saw that I had done badly on it, I was so upset that I locked myself in the bathroom and cried. I hid the test and never told my parents about it. After that I worked even harder.

The best thing that happened to me that year was meeting Suni. It happened about three quarters of the way through the year. I was moved into a higher math class, and my seat was right next to Suni. When I realized she could speak Chinese, I was incredibly happy. Suni was really friendly, so I wasn't embarrassed to ask her for help with my English.

After that, school wasn't so bad. My English improved, and my grades got better. But then in the last weeks of school that year, something happened that made me see that no matter how well I do or how hard I try, there are some people in this country who will never accept me. I wrote a report on Chinese immigrants for social studies. My teacher was so impressed with it that she asked me to read it to the class. I practiced reading it a hundred times in front of the mirror. I read it to Suni, and she said it was perfect.

I was so nervous as I walked up to the front of the room, praying that my English would not fail me. My mouth was dry, but I read the report and it went fine. When I finished, I looked at Suni, and she put her thumb and finger together in the sign meaning great. I was so happy and proud until a classmate named Sheila Benson ruined it all for me. As I walked by her desk toward the back of the classroom she whispered, "If it's so hard, why didn't you stay in China, slant eyes?" Then she spit on my paper. I'll never forget the look of pure hatred on her face.

I never told my parents or my teacher about that incident.

I never told anyone, not even Suni or Melissa. I was too ashamed. You might say that Sheila Benson should have been ashamed, not me, and in my head I knew that. But in my heart I knew that I would never forget the way Sheila looked at me, or what she did to me.

Yes, today I want to say to my mother, I know about prejudice. I know about hatred. But I'm not going to hide in my house because of it. There may be some people who hate me, but there are also plenty who like me, and I'm going to be with them. My parents have to accept that. I'm going to Michael's party no matter what.

On Friday, I took my party clothes to school with me so I could change at Suni's house. Actually I couldn't decide what to wear, so I took two outfits. That night Suni and I dressed for the party up in her room, and I tried on both outfits. The first was a pair of wide-leg black pants that I had made, with a white blouse and a suede vest I found in a thrift shop. The second outfit was a long black tunic top over a short denim skirt. Finally I decided to wear the denim skirt with the shirt and vest, and Suni borrowed the tunic top to wear with her jeans.

I was putting on some lipstick when we heard a horn blow from outside. Suni ran to the window. "That's them," she said. She stopped for one last look in the mirror. "Do I look okay?" she asked.

"You look great. I love those earrings," I told her.

"You look great too. That vest is fantastic." She grabbed my hand and we ran downstairs.

"Bye, Mom!" she shouted.

"Have fun, girls," said Mrs. Tabor.

Melissa and her boyfriend, Alex, waved as we came down the walk. Suni opened the back door of the car and slid in, and I climbed in next to her.

"This is so cool. I can't believe you're allowed to come," Melissa said when she saw me.

"Well, actually I'm not. They think we're just having dinner at Suni's house. If they found out we were going to Michael's . . . oh, I don't even want to think about it."

"Then don't. They won't find out, and anyway, what are they going to do about it? Call the National Guard?" Melissa said.

"How many people are coming?" Suni asked.

"I don't think even Michael knows, but it's going to be big," Alex said.

"He always has great parties," Suni added.

Melissa turned back in her seat and said, "You look so good, An-ying. I want that vest. Where'd you get it?"

"Reruns," I told her. "You know, that secondhand shop on Elmhurst? I find a lot of stuff in there. The bottom of this was all frayed, but I sewed on a border to make it look okay."

"Okay? I'd kill for a vest like that. I saw one almost like it at Mondo's, but it would have cost my next ten paychecks, so I couldn't get it." Melissa has a job scooping ice cream at Sundae's Ice Cream and Yogurt Shop. She works three days a week after school, from four to nine.

I was glad I had decided to wear the vest. I knew it looked good, and as nervous as I was feeling, I needed all the help I could get. Suni and Melissa went to parties like this all the time, but for me it was new.

As we turned onto Michael's street we could hear music, and the noise of the party spilled out of his house. It was a warm night for October, and groups of kids were hanging around outside on the lawn and near the front steps. The moon was full and a soft breeze was blowing, but it wasn't at all cold.

"It's a perfect night for a party," I said.

"Last year it rained and everyone was squashed in the basement. This will be better," Suni agreed.

Alex found a parking spot up the street, and the four of us climbed out. As we walked toward Michael's house, Alex took Melissa's hand and pulled her back. "You guys go on. We'll meet you in there," he said. I turned to say something, but they were so engrossed in making out that I didn't bother.

"Well, that's the last we'll see of them till it's time to go home," said Suni. "They're so wrapped up in each other, you have to wonder why they even came to the party."

Suni and I walked down the block toward Michael's house. The music was blaring, and people were talking and laughing. Some kids were sitting in a circle on the edge of the lawn, and one of them called to Suni. We went over to the group, and one of the guys reached up and took Suni's hand. "Suni, where've you been? I've been waiting all night for you."

Suni laughed. "It's eight-thirty, Jeff. The party just started, and you're already wasted." Suni looked at me and rolled her eyes.

"Me? Wasted? Bite your tongue." He took my hand with his other one and tried to pull both of us down. "Sit down. Don't go in there. There's nothing but a bunch of sweaty people dancing. Much nicer out here."

"We're going to go in to get a soda. We'll come back, okay? Come on," she said to me, and I followed her up the walk.

"God. What an idiot," she whispered when we were out of earshot.

Suni led me inside and down to the basement. I wondered where Michael's parents were, and if they were even home. I thought about what my parents would do if I ever had a party like this, and I laughed out loud at the thought.

"What?" asked Suni.

"Nothing. I was just thinking about what my parents would say about something like this."

"Don't even think about it," she replied. "There are some drinks. You want a Coke?"

I followed her across the room to a table that held soft drinks, ice, chips, and pretzels.

Suni and I poured Cokes and then looked around. There were a few familiar faces, kids I had seen at school, but no one I knew very well. I saw Suni anxiously searching the room, and I figured she was looking for Jason Thorndike. I knew she was hoping he'd be here. Suddenly she grabbed my arm and squeezed. "There he is," she whispered.

"Where?"

"Shhh. Don't look. I don't want him to think I'm

looking for him." Suni turned around and faced the table at the same time I noticed Jason coming toward us. He was tall, with a thin, bony face and dark brown hair that he wore long and parted in the middle. "He's coming," I whispered to Suni, and in a minute he was standing behind us.

"Hi, An-ying. Hi, Suni." He had to shout to be heard over the music.

Suni whirled around. "Oh, hi, Jason. I didn't know you were going to be here." She was trying to sound casual, but I knew she was so nervous that her knees were shaking. She'd had a crush on this guy for months, and this was practically the first time he had actually talked to her.

"Yeah. I've known Michael for a long time. We're both on the swim team." We could hardly hear him over the party noise.

"It's really hot in here. Want to go outside?" he asked.

Suni looked at me. "Want to?"

I nodded, and we followed Jason back up the stairs and out of the house. Now there were even more kids outside, some standing, some sitting in groups on the lawn. Jason, Suni, and I sat on the front steps. Jason and Suni began to talk about their chemistry teacher, while I just watched the party happen around me. I was glad to be there, but I was beginning to feel out of place. It seemed as though everyone was with someone, a boyfriend or girlfriend.

They all seemed so confident, like they belonged

there. Most of them probably went to parties like this every weekend.

We sat there for a while, and then Suni said, “We’re going to look for Chris and Tina. Want to come?”

I shook my head, smiling at Suni. “See you later.” She gave my shoulder a squeeze as they went off, and I knew she was so happy to be with Jason. When they left, I was all alone, wondering what to do. Should I go look for Alex and Melissa, or go back downstairs? I didn’t want to face the crowd and the noise of the basement, and I was pretty sure Alex and Melissa wanted to be alone, but I felt stupid sitting there all by myself. I looked out across the lawn and saw the other groups of kids talking and laughing. Maybe I should have listened to my mother and stayed home. Maybe she was right. Chinese girls don’t belong at parties like this.

There was only one other person who was alone. He was leaning against a car parked in the drive on the side of the house, holding a can of soda. I noticed him because he seemed to be watching me. It made me nervous. He had light brown or dirty blond hair, I couldn’t tell which in the light, and it was pulled back into a ponytail. He was tall and thin, and looked older than the other guys at the party.

Finally I decided to go back in the house. I stood up and was about to open the door when there was a loud noise from inside. The door flew open and a boy came bombing out. He ran smack into me, and I almost fell down the steps. He must have been mad about something because he didn't bother to apologize but sort of scowled at me and pushed past me. Before I knew what happened, the boy with the ponytail grabbed the other boy and said, "Watch it. You almost knocked her over."

"Hey, you watch it, man," the other boy mumbled, shaking his arm free. "It was an accident, okay?" He glared at the boy with the ponytail, and then went on down the steps to join a group sitting at the other end of the lawn.

"Are you okay?" the boy asked me.

"I'm fine," I said. "I . . . I was just going inside."

"Wait . . . I, ah . . . I noticed you sitting here, and I was just about to come and talk to you when that bozo crashed into you."

So he had noticed that I was sitting alone, that I had no one to talk to. He probably could see how out of place I was. He probably wondered what I was even doing here.

"I don't know too many people here," I said.

"That's great!" he said. "Neither do I. Well, it's not great . . . I mean . . ."

I laughed.

"Let me start over," he said. "What I meant is, you look like someone I'd like to get to know."

"Oh." I studied him for a minute. I liked his looks. There was something about him that seemed real. He didn't seem to be playing any kind of role.

He swept his arm toward his car. "Can I offer you a spot on my car? You get a great view of the party from there."

I decided it was better than going inside or sitting there alone, so I said okay and followed him to the car beside the house. We sat on the hood and he said, "My name's Joey Shelton."

"I'm An-ying Chang."

"Do you go to Franklin?" he asked.

I nodded. "I'm a senior. How about you?"

"I graduated from Stuyvesant last year."

"How do you know Michael?"

"We work together at Sound Waves. It's a music store on Forty-ninth Street."

He took a long drink of his soda, tilting back his head and finishing it off. He set the empty bottle down on the wall beside him. "So you graduate in June?" he asked.

I nodded again. "Unless I really screw up between now and then."

He smiled. "You won't."

"No. I'll graduate."

"Then what?"

I shrugged. "College, I hope."

"Do you know where?"

"I'd like to go to Wharton. In Philadelphia."

"Wharton? Uh-oh. Now I'm starting to get intimidated. Maybe I should go home and start reading my dictionary or something."

I laughed. "So you work at Sound Waves? Do you like it?"

He shrugged. "It's a job. I like being around music. I get to hear everything new that comes out, and I get a discount on anything I buy. I wouldn't want to do it for the rest of my life, but it's okay for now." He picked up a leaf that had fallen on the car and twirled it between his fingers. "I like my other job better, but it doesn't pay enough right now."

"What's your other job?"

"I'm a sound mixer at a recording studio. Well, I'm learning to be one. Right now I'm really more of a gofer than anything else, but it's a good way to learn the business."

I didn't know what a sound mixer was, and I didn't want to seem dumb, so I decided the safest thing to do was change the subject. "Is this your own car?"

He shook his head. "My dad's. I live in the city now, so I don't need one. Can't afford one, either. My parents let me borrow theirs sometimes on weekends."

"Do you have an apartment?" I asked.

He nodded. "On Forty-third between Eighth and Ninth. I share it with three other guys. It's kind of a zoo, but it's better than living at home."

"It sounds fun, though. I can't wait till I can move away from home."

"You don't get along with your parents?"

I sighed. How could I explain my parents to him? "Let's just say we have a small communication problem. Actually, a big communication problem."

"It's funny. Now that I have my own place, I get along okay with my parents. I even stay there on weekends sometimes. But living with them? No way."

"Where do they live?" I asked.

"Brooklyn. Not far from here. How about you?"

"Same. We live on Carlyle Street."

"Were you born in Brooklyn?"

I smiled. "I was born in Hong Kong."

He looked surprised. "Really?"

"We came here when I was ten."

"Wow. I thought it was a big deal moving from Brooklyn to the city, but Hong Kong to Brooklyn? That's a few zip codes, at least."

I laughed.

"What?" he asked.

"You're just funny."

He scratched at something on the hood of the car and then looked at me with a smile. "I guess that was sort of a stupid statement," he said.

"Not stupid. Just funny."

I don't know how long we had been talking when Melissa and Alex came out of the house. "I found her, you guys. Over there," I heard Melissa say, and Suni appeared behind her. The three of them crossed the lawn and Melissa said, "It's almost eleven-thirty. We've got to get going." She looked at Joey. I introduced them, and we slid off the car. Joey walked with the rest of us to Alex's car. While Alex unlocked the doors, Joey said, "Umm, listen. I'd like to see you again. Can I give you a call or something?"

I felt a mixture of panic and relief. I had been hoping he would ask, but if he called me at home, what would my parents say? I gave him my phone number anyway, and he wrote it on a scrap of paper he found in his pocket.

I got into the backseat next to Melissa, and as he shut the car door he said, "I'll call you."

"He's cute," said Suni as we drove off. "I've never seen him before. Is he a friend of Michael's?"

"He works with him at Sound Waves," I said.

"Does he go to Franklin?" asked Melissa.

"No. Stuyvesant. He graduated last year. He wants to be a sound mixer. Does anyone know what a sound mixer is?"

"Yeah. It's a guy who mixes sound," said Alex.

"Thanks a lot."

"Well, do you really want to know?" he asked. Alex plays bass guitar.

"Yes," I said.

He launched into this long explanation of exactly what a sound mixer does. Finally Melissa said, "Enough already. She just wanted to know what it is. She doesn't want a three-hour lecture."

"Did you have fun with Jason?" I asked Suni.

She nodded happily. "Can you believe it? I swear I've dreamed about this for months, and now it's actually happened. I was with him all night. He said he'll call me tomorrow."

I was happy for Suni. And I was feeling just as excited about Joey.

It was eleven-forty by the time Alex stopped in front of my house. I thanked everyone as I climbed out and hurried up my front walk. I hoped my parents would be asleep, but I saw a light on in the living room, so I knew one of them would be waiting up for me. As I reached for the doorknob my mother opened it.

"Shemma bende ren!" she said. "What kind of fool are you? Do you know what time it is?"

"I know. I'm sorry, Ma. We all got talking after dinner at Suni's and just sort of lost track of the time."

My mother shook her head, but before she could say any more, I said, "I'm really tired. I'm going up to bed."

I don't know if she believed me or not, but I didn't care. I was glad I had gone to the party, and glad that I had met Joey. I fell asleep wondering if he really would call, and hoping that he would.

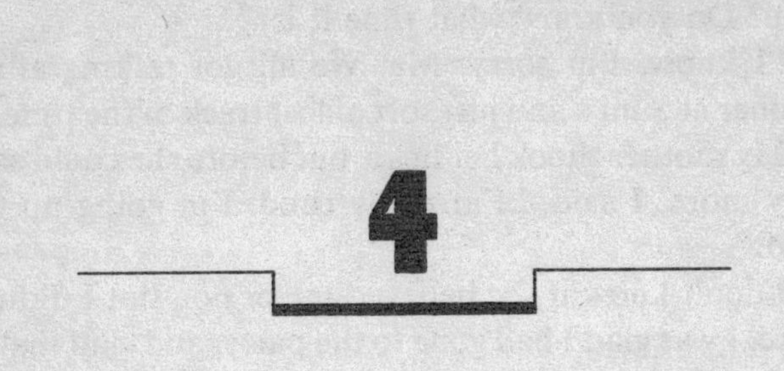

The next night I got to my aunt's house at exactly six-thirty. I made sure I was right on time, and I even stopped on the way over and bought her a little bouquet of flowers. Aunt Su-lin is funny. She's really moody, and you're never quite sure what to expect from her. If she gets mad at you for some reason, some little thing you did but you didn't even know you did, she can be very mean, and sometimes she won't speak to you for days. I remember once when she came to our house for dinner and by mistake my mother served my aunt last. My aunt wouldn't speak to her for two weeks. Anyway, this time I wanted to make sure my aunt was in a good mood so I could get her on my side about going to Wharton.

When I got to her house, she gave me with a big hug and seemed really happy to see me.

"Oh," she said after we hugged. "I haven't seen you in ages. Look at this new haircut. So stylish! I know your mother hates it, but I kind of like it. It suits you."

"That's what all my friends say."

"Well, we have lots to talk about. You sit right here while I get a vase for these beautiful flowers, and then we'll catch up. Dinner's all cooked. We'll eat in few minutes."

Before my aunt went to the kitchen, she went back to the window and looked out. I thought maybe she was watching for my uncle, but then I remembered she said he'd be at a meeting.

While she was in the kitchen, I looked around. My aunt loves pretty things and spends lots of time decorating. I noticed that she made a new cover for the sofa, a bright, flowery chintz, and I called to her that I liked it. The room was bright and airy, full of pastels and flowers. A room that reflected my aunt much more than my uncle. I looked at the photographs on the table beside the sofa. There was one of me that had been taken two years earlier. I was dressed in one of my old dresses, one that my mother made me, and my hair was long and pulled back. I looked so much younger. I stood up and went to the mirror. I hardly looked like the same girl. Had I really changed that much in two years?

My aunt came back with the flowers in a vase and a plate of crackers, which she placed on the coffee table.

Before she sat down, she looked at her watch, and then went to the window again.

"Are you waiting for my uncle? I thought you said he was at a meeting."

"That's right. He has a business meeting tonight, so it's just us. We can really have a good talk."

She came and sat down on the other side of the sofa and turned to me. "So tell me what you've been doing. Are you studying and sewing all the time? I hope you have a chance to have a little fun with your friends now and then."

"I wish you'd tell my mother that. She thinks all I should do is work."

Aunt Su looked thoughtful. "She worries about you, that's all. It's not easy to be a mother, you know."

"I know, but sometimes she worries too much. She thinks I'm still a kid. I've grown up a lot in the last few years." I picked up the picture of me from the coffee table. "Look at this," I said. "That's not me anymore."

My aunt took a cracker and nibbled it absently. She offered the plate to me, and I took one. She kept looking at her watch as we talked.

"Well, you'll be graduating in June. Things will be different then. Do you have any plans for next year?"

"Actually, that's one of the things I wanted to talk to you about. Remember I told you about Ms. Brady, my math teacher and also my adviser?"

"Ms. Brady? Yes, I remember you told me about her. But I hope you're not planning to ask me anything about math. You showed me your math book once and I thought I was looking at a foreign language. It made no sense to me. And to be honest, I'm really not sure why they have to teach all those things, allergies and geology and all that."

"You mean algebra and geometry, Aunty."

"Yes, well, whatever. Do you really need to know all that?" Aunt Su looked at her watch again and then jumped up from the sofa and went to the window, looking out at the street.

"Are you waiting for someone, Aunty?" I asked her again.

"Waiting? No, no, I was just checking to see if the rain had started yet. It's supposed to rain tonight, you know."

"It is? I hadn't heard."

My aunt came back to the sofa and perched on the arm beside me. She ran her hand through my short hair. "So stylish you are these days. I bet the boys your age love it."

"I guess they like it okay," I said. I didn't really know what to say to that. Why was she asking me about boys? I wished she would just sit still and listen to me tell her my problem. "Anyway," I went on. "I was telling you about Ms. Brady. She said she's almost sure I can get a full scholarship—"

Before I could finish, the doorbell rang and my aunt jumped up and rushed to answer it. "Who in the world could that be?" she said.

My aunt opened the door and exclaimed, "Why,

Paul! How are you? Come in, come in. What a coincidence. Isn't this great."

She ushered in a Chinese boy who looked about my age. "Look, An-ying. Look who it is. It's Paul Chun. Isn't this a surprise?"

"You did say Saturday at six-thirty, didn't you, Mrs. Wong?" he asked.

"Did I?" My aunt looked nervously at me. "I guess I did. It must have slipped my mind. I'm forgetting everything lately. Old age, I guess. But you children don't have to worry about that." She pushed Paul toward the sofa and said, "Here's my niece, An-ying Chang. An-ying, this is Paul Chun, the son of a very good friend of mine." Aunt Su-lin stood beaming at us and then said, "Why don't you two sit and get acquainted while I see about dinner?"

"Let me help you, Aunt Su," I said, jumping up and following my aunt to the kitchen.

When the kitchen door closed, I planted myself in front of my aunt, who was standing by the open refrigerator. "You didn't tell me you asked anyone else. I thought it was going to be only you and me."

"I told you I just forgot, dear." She lowered her voice and whispered, "But he is such a nice boy. I showed him a picture of you a few weeks ago, and he's been dying to meet you ever since. Now that he's here, why don't you just try to get to know him? Like I said, you work too hard. You need to have a little fun, meet some boys your own age."

I knew my aunt had planned the whole thing, and I

was so furious I could barely speak. The idea that she would interfere in my life like this made me so angry I felt like leaving right then and there. I wanted to tell her that I could plan my own life and make my own friends, and I didn't need her help. I guess she could tell by looking at me that I was mad, because she said, "Now, An-ying. Maybe I should have warned you, but Paul is so nice, and I only wanted the two of you to meet." She put a hand on either side of my face. "You're such a beautiful girl. I just want the best for you. Please, be nice. Just go talk to him. It won't hurt you."

I took a deep breath and went out of the kitchen back to the living room, where Paul was sitting stiffly on the couch.

"So where do you go to school?" I asked him as I sat down.

"Jenkins. I'm a senior. How about you?"

"Franklin. I'm a senior too." I passed him the tray of crackers, and he took one. For a minute neither of us said anything, and then we both spoke at once.

"Sorry," he said. "Go ahead."

"I was just going to ask if you know what you want to do after graduation." I sounded so boring. It was so awkward. Why had my aunt arranged this? The more I thought about it, the madder I got.

"College, I hope. I've applied to NYU and Columbia. How about you? Your aunt told me you get straight A's."

I rolled my eyes. "My aunt talks too much."

He laughed. "She was really determined that I meet you."

"What do you mean?"

He shrugged. "Just that she and my mother have been on the phone constantly, trying to arrange this."

"You mean you didn't ask to meet me?"

"Well, not really. Your aunt showed me your picture and told me all about you, and then she said, 'You have to meet her. I'll work it out.' "

"My aunt told me that she showed you my picture and you were dying to meet me."

Paul blushed and said, "Well, I did . . . I mean, I do think you're really pretty, but the truth is, I already have a girlfriend. I was supposed to meet her tonight, but my mother made me come here."

"Ohhh. This makes me so mad." I held my face in my hands, my eyes closed. "I'm sorry." I looked up at him. "I'm not mad at you. Just at my aunt. Why does she have to try to run my life?"

"My mother's the same way. Actually, this might have been her idea. You probably shouldn't blame your aunt."

"What do they think? Do they really think they can control us like this?"

He shrugged. "Who knows? All I know is that sometimes it's easier just to go along with it than to try to fight it."

Even though I was so mad I felt like screaming at my aunt, I knew he was right. There was no point in trying to fight it. If I made a big scene now, my aunt would never forgive me, and I still wanted to get her on my side about Wharton. Then I had an idea. "Listen," I said. "Maybe we can work this out. Call your girlfriend and tell her you'll meet her at eight. I'll tell my aunt you're going to walk me home. That way we can at least get out of here early, and my aunt and your mother will be happy."

"Really?"

"Why not? Why should we both be miserable . . . I mean, not miserable, but . . ."

He nodded. "I know what you mean."

While he was on the phone, I went back to the kitchen and told my aunt that Paul seemed nice. The rest of the dinner was pleasant enough, and when Paul and I left together, I could see my aunt was pleased. As soon as we got to the end of the block Paul said, "I don't mind walking you home."

"That's okay. I'll just say good-bye here." I put out my hand and he shook it.

"Thanks," he said. "It really was good to meet you. I hope I see you again sometime."

"Me too," I said. And I meant it.

The next day was Sunday, and I had a lot of homework to do. I sat in my room trying to concentrate, but I kept thinking about Joey. No matter how hard I tried, I couldn't get him out of my mind. I kept remembering the way he smiled, and the way he looked at me as if he was really interested in what I was saying. When the phone rang, I raced down the hall to get it, but my mother got it first. She handed me the receiver, and I took a big breath before I said hello. When I heard his voice, my heart started pounding and my mouth went dry.

"An-ying?"

"Yes."

"This is Joey Shelton."

"Right. Hi."

"I wondered if you wanted to do something soon. A movie or something."

"Yeah, that'd be great."

"Okay. How about Friday?"

"Umm, okay. I think Friday's good." God, I sounded so stupid. And I didn't know what I was going to tell my parents. I would have to meet him somewhere—he couldn't come to the house.

"Okay. How about if I call later in the week and we'll figure what to see and all?"

"Sounds like a plan," I said.

We said good-bye and hung up, and I wished that I had said something interesting instead of sounding like a total idiot.

I hurried back to my room so my mother wouldn't corner me with a list of questions, but that night at dinner, before I even took one bite, she said, "And who was that who called you earlier? Some boy whose voice I did not recognize."

I wanted to tell her it was none of her business, but I knew that would just make her angry, so I made up another lie. "It was just a boy from school. He wanted to know something about the math homework."

I don't know if my mother believed me or not, but at least she didn't ask me any more questions. I was surprised at how easy it was becoming to lie to her. I wished I didn't have to, but I wasn't going to give up my chance to see Joey.

5

It was Monday night. My parents, Lee, and I were just sitting down for dinner when we heard the front door open and Ben's voice saying, "Straight ahead, down the stairs." Through the doorway between the dining room and the front hall I saw two guys go past and start downstairs. Ben followed them, shouting, "Hello, everyone!" to us as he passed.

As I watched them go by I thought that it was a good thing my father's back was to them because they didn't exactly look like his idea of the perfect guests. The first one was short and fat and wore a black leather jacket and tight black jeans. His head was shaved on one side, and his hair hung long and greasy on the other. The other one looked a bit older. He wore sunglasses, even though it had been dark for an hour.

"Nice little playmates Ben's bringing home these days," Lee said.

My mother just looked at him and shook her head. I knew she and my father were both worried about Ben, but had no idea what to do. My father picked up his fork, then frowned and put it down again. He looked at my mother. "I thought he was job hunting."

My mother stared at her plate. Obviously hoping to change the subject, she said, "Lee, how was your history test? Did you do all right?"

Lee shrugged. "It was okay, except Mr. Bradford gave some questions we never even talked about. He's so unfair."

I laughed. Lee was always complaining about how unfair his teachers were.

"Well, he is. He's always throwing in questions about stuff we never talked about in class."

"You could try reading your assignments," I said.

"I did. I swear, we never studied half of what was on the test. He had this question about—" He stopped when we heard shouting coming from downstairs. "Jeez. What's going on down there?" he asked.

We all sat in silence, listening to the sounds from Ben's room. There was more shouting, and then a crash. Then there was deadly silence in the house. My parents looked at each other, concern and fear on my mother's face, anger on my father's.

My father threw down his napkin and got up from

the table. He went to the top of the stairs and called, "Ben, what's going on?"

There was no answer. A minute later the two guys came thumping up the steps, pushed past my father, and went out the front door. My father rushed after them and shouted in Chinese at them to stay out of his house, to stay in the gutter where they belonged.

"Maybe it's a good thing Dad never learned to speak English," Lee said. I knew he was joking, but really, I thought, it was true. From the looks of those two they might have beaten him up if they had understood what he was saying. Dad slammed the door, went back to the stairs, and shouted down to my brother, "Ben-li, come up here, please. I wish to speak to you."

"Relax, Dad. I'll be up in a minute."

"Not in a minute. I said now."

"Jeez. Take it easy, man," Ben said as he came upstairs. "Sorry about the noise. We had a little disagreement. Nothing to worry about." Ben's lower lip was swollen and bloody, and he held a red bandanna against it to stop the bleeding. He loaded a plate of food from the stove and came to the table.

"Those two are not welcome here ever again," my father said. "They are lowlife. Why do you associate with lowlife?"

"They're just a couple of guys I met at work," Ben mumbled.

"At work? Ha. You haven't had a job in months. What work is this?"

Ben slammed his fist on the table. "Look, man, just stay off my case! I don't need this, all right?"

Ben and my father glared at each other. My father's face turned pale. He had never looked so angry. For a minute I thought he was going to hit Ben.

Finally Ben said, "Look, I'm sorry. Okay?"

My father said nothing but slowly picked up his fork and went back to his dinner. My mother looked close to tears. Everyone was silent. I didn't feel like eating anymore.

Ben ate quickly, shoveling the food into his mouth as if he couldn't wait to be done. When he was finished, he picked up his plate and took it to the kitchen. On his way through the dining room he said to Lee, "Come downstairs after dinner. I've got something for you."

When Ben left the room, the rest of us relaxed a bit. "Good dinner, Ma," Lee said. Then he began telling a long story about how unfair his biology teacher was. Ma tried to look as if she was listening, but I could see that she was still upset by Ben. If only he could get a job, I thought, and get his life back on track.

Two hours later I was up in my room doing homework when Lee came in. "Look at this," he said, holding out his wrist. On it was a brand-new watch that looked expensive.

"Where'd you get it?" I asked, already knowing the answer.

"Ben gave it to me," he said happily. "Isn't it cool? It's got a calendar, a timer, and an alarm."

"That's cool," I said. But all I could think of was how Ben paid for it. Or my new Walkman, and all the new clothes Ben had been wearing lately. Expensive stuff, like his leather jacket. For someone who was out of work, he sure had a lot of cash.

Lee sat on the bed, fiddling with his watch.

"Did Ben say where he got it?" I asked.

"He has money left over from when he was working," Lee said. "He made a lot at that job. And he told me he might get a good new job soon. He said he's almost sure it's going to work out."

"Yeah, well, I hope it does."

Lee sounded so hopeful, but I knew he was just as concerned as I was about Ben. Lee has always idolized him.

After Lee left, I decided I would try to talk to Ben to find out what was going on. I went downstairs to his room. He was lying on his bed with headphones on. When he saw me, he took them off and said, "Hey, what's up? Did Lee show you the watch I gave him? He was pretty excited about it."

I nodded as I sat down on the end of his bed. "It's really nice," I said. "Too nice. You know he'll probably break it or lose it in a week."

Ben shrugged. "How's that Walkman I gave you? Good sound?"

"Great. But I'm wondering where you get the money for all this stuff. I mean, it's all expensive. How can you afford it?"

"I had some cash left over from when I was working, and I'm just about to get a job unloading trucks. It'll be hard work, but big bucks. I figure if I'm going to be busting my hump I might as well get some enjoyment out of it."

"But a month ago you told me you were flat broke. And you haven't been working since then, so where'd the money come from?"

Ben sat up. I could tell he was annoyed. "Look," he said, "it's my business where my money comes from. It's my money, and I'll spend it any way I want, okay?"

"Okay, but . . ."

"But what?"

"I just hope you're not doing something . . ."

"Something like what?"

"I don't know. Something illegal or something."

"God, you're as bad as Ma and Dad," Ben said. He stood up and walked over to the closet. "I wish everyone around here would let me run my own life. I get really sick of everyone trying to tell me what to do." As he said it he yanked open the door of the closet and grabbed his leather jacket.

"But those guys, Ben, the ones who came over tonight. Who were they?"

"Look, An-ying. I told you to stay out of my business. I can take care of myself. I don't need my little sister worrying about me." He put on his jacket and turned angrily to me. "You sit there in your safe little high school world, thinking you'll go to college and everything will be fine. But there's a lot you don't know about the rest of the world. Not everything is fair. Not everything works the way you think it should. Sometimes you have to take things into your own hands. I'm not going to sit around broke and begging for work from some creep when there are other ways to get money. And I'm not going to explain myself to you. It's my business. Mine. So you and Ma and Dad can just stay out of it."

He pushed past me and stomped upstairs. I heard the front door slam, and I wished I had kept my mouth shut.

Later, as I lay in bed trying to fall asleep, I listened, hoping to hear his footsteps coming up the stairs, but I fell asleep still waiting. The next morning, as soon as I was dressed, I decided I would go to his room to apologize. I knew how it felt, having people watching every move you make and worrying about you, the way Ma and Dad did with me. I didn't want to do that to him. I felt bad that I pried into his life last night, and I wanted to tell him so. I wanted to explain that it was just because I cared about him.

I went downstairs to Ben's room and knocked on his door. There was no answer, so I figured he was asleep, which didn't surprise me since I knew he had been out so late. I pushed open the door and looked in. His bed was made, his room empty. Ben hadn't come home last night.

When I got home from school that afternoon, my mother was sitting in the kitchen, stringing snow peas. When she looked up at me, I could see she had been crying, though she tried to hide it.

"Ben's still not home?" I asked her.

She shook her head.

"Did he call or anything?"

She shook her head again.

"Have you called any of his friends? Maybe Tom Ling knows where he is."

"Tom Ling is away at college. Ben hasn't seen him in months. I don't know who his friends are nowadays. I don't even know who to call."

I sat down at the table and began helping my mother with the snow peas. "Don't worry, Ma. I'm sure he's all right. He probably just fell asleep at a friend's house. He'll be home soon."

We waited all afternoon and evening. Every time there was a noise outside, my mother went to the window to see if it was Ben, but it never was. At dinner my parents discussed what to do. My mother said, "I think we have to go to the police. We don't know where he is. He could be hurt, or . . . who knows where he might be."

"No," my father said. "We do not go to the police. We don't need the police to help. This is a private matter. He will turn up. Or I will find him myself." He was worried about the family's reputation.

My mother said nothing.

I thought, How is my father going to find Ben when he can't even speak English? I decided to look for Ben if he wasn't home by tomorrow. I knew he hung out in Chinatown. I had heard him talking about a place called the Orient Grill. I decided I would start to look for him there.

I knew my parents would never allow me to go to Chinatown alone, so once again I made up a lie.

"Listen, Ma," I said. "I've got a big history project coming up. I'm going to go to the library tomorrow afternoon and get started, so don't expect me home right after school."

"Okay, but no later than six o'clock, you hear?"

I nodded. It was my fault that Ben had taken off. I had to find him.

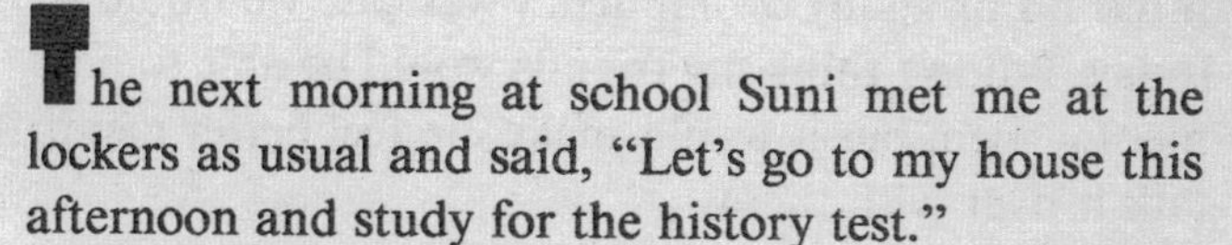

The next morning at school Suni met me at the lockers as usual and said, "Let's go to my house this afternoon and study for the history test."

"Um, I can't."

"Why? Your parents didn't find out about Michael's, did they?"

"No. Ma was a little suspicious, but she didn't say anything. I just have something else to do."

Suni gave me a puzzled look. "Like what?"

I wanted to tell her about Ben, but I knew my parents would kill me if I told anyone. I hesitated, and she looked at me, frowning as she does when she's thinking about something. "Hey, you look like you haven't slept in weeks," she said. "Is something wrong? I thought everything was great. Especially since you met Joey. Did you have a fight with him or something?"

I shook my head. I had to tell Suni. I couldn't keep it inside. "No. It's Ben." Before I could say any more, the bell rang. "I'll tell you at lunch."

"Okay. Let's go to the deli. I'll tell Melissa in math."

There's a deli on the corner two blocks from school. Because we're seniors, we're allowed to leave campus during lunch break, so a few times a week the three of us walk down there for lunch, especially when we have something to talk over. Melissa and Suni buy lunch there, but I usually bring my own sandwich so I don't have to buy one. Everyone who works at the deli is nice, and as long as I buy a drink there, they don't mind if I bring my own lunch. I was glad we would go today. I didn't think my friends would be able to help me find Ben, but it would make me feel better just to talk it over with them.

The morning seemed to last a decade, but at last the bell rang for lunch. We met again by the lockers. Since I have math right across the hall, I was the first to get there. After I put my books away and took out my jacket, I heard Melissa. She slammed her locker door and said, "God, I hate her."

"Who?" I asked as I came around the row of lockers to where hers was.

"Take a wild guess."

I knew she was talking about Madame Demoise, her French teacher.

"The woman is sick, I tell you, sick. If everyone in the class flunks a test, you'd think she might figure out that maybe, just maybe, there's a problem with her teaching, wouldn't you? But no. She couldn't possibly be the one with the problem."

"Everyone flunked the test?"

"Well, everyone except Marci Rytter and Jeffrey Heiner. Marci's never gotten less than an A in her life, and Jeffrey Heiner speaks French practically as well as he speaks English. He shouldn't be in our class. It's not fair. Why did my parents force me to take honors track French? If I'd known I was going to have Madame Wacko for a teacher, I would never have done it."

Suni appeared in the middle of this tirade, and the three of us headed for the deli.

"Did I tell you what she said to me yesterday?" Melissa went on. Suni looked at me, rolled her eyes, and said, "I guess she needs to vent. What did she say to you yesterday, Melissa?"

"Well, I told you she wrote on my last paper that I should participate more in class. So I'm trying to participate more, raising my hand all the time, answering lots of questions. So yesterday she says, 'You talk too much. Let someone else have a chance.'" Melissa threw up her hands and shook her head. "I tell you, the woman's nuts. Probably dangerous."

When Melissa finally ran out of steam, Suni said, "Well, now that that's out of the way, tell us about Ben, An-ying. What happened?"

"I don't know, really, but the night before last we had a fight, and he left the house. That's the last we've seen of him."

"What were you fighting about?" Suni asked.

"Well, it wasn't a fight, exactly. He just got mad because he thought I was prying into his life." Melissa had taken off her glasses and was chewing on one earpiece. She did this a lot when she was listening. Suni was watching me too, waiting for me to go on. At first I wasn't going to tell them everything, but now I wanted to.

"Listen, if I tell you what I know, you have to promise not to tell a soul. My parents would kill me if they find out I've talked to anyone about this. They've got this thing about family pride, you know."

They promised not to tell anyone, and I told them how moody Ben had been lately, and about the phone calls and the weird guys who had come to the house. I even told them about all the stuff he'd been buying.

"So you think Ben is mixed up in something illegal?" Suni asked. "Drugs?"

"I don't know, but . . . I just wish I knew where he was. I did this—I made him mad. That's why I have to find him."

"So what are you going to do?" asked Melissa.

"I'm going to Chinatown today to look for him after school."

"Why Chinatown?" asked Suni.

"I know he hangs out there a lot. I've heard him mention a place called the Orient Grill. Maybe he's there."

"I can come with you if you want," Suni said.

"Me too," said Melissa.

"Thanks, you guys, but I think I'd better go alone. I'll have better luck getting information if it's just me."

"But be careful," Suni said. "Hey, you know Brad Hsu? He's a senior and in my history class."

"Yeah, I know Brad. He was in my biology class last year."

"Well, he works in Chinatown. At a restaurant. The Red Dragon, I think he said. Maybe he could help."

I nodded. "I'll talk to him."

As we finished our lunches Suni said, "Do you remember back in tenth grade when I was in love with Ben? God, I thought he was so handsome. And he never even noticed me. I was just his kid sister's friend. And when he started dating that Alison Song, I was so jealous. Remember?"

I smiled. Lots of girls had their eye on Ben. He used to always have girls calling him.

"What ever happened to Alison?" Suni asked.

"She's away at college now. A lot of Ben's friends are."

"It's kind of scary to think that next year at this time we'll be away at college," Suni said. "Or whatever."

"I guess," I said. I thought college sounded less scary than a night in Chinatown or life with my parents.

We finished our lunches and headed back to school. I had a lot of trouble concentrating the rest of the afternoon, and when the bell finally rang, I was anxious to get going. I didn't know exactly how I would go about finding Ben, but I knew I had to try.

In the subway on the way to Chinatown, I kept thinking about Ben when he was younger. I missed how close we had been. When we first got to New York, Ben was so happy. I remembered how excited he was when he got his first glimpse of the Statue of Liberty. Ben and I spent a lot of time alone together in those first years, when my parents were always at work. I had a lot of studying to do every day, but Ben usually tried to talk me out of it. He always had something he wanted me to do with him.

I remembered the apartment building we lived in the first two years in New York. Ben and I used to sneak up onto the roof of the building until we got caught by the landlord. And we used to spy on the other people in the building. Ben could always come up with ideas for fun things to do.

He never did much schoolwork, and he never could understand why I bothered. He managed to pass most of his courses, but just barely. My parents were relieved when he finally graduated.

A tall woman with long red hair got on the subway car a few stops after me, and I began to play my favorite game. I play it whenever I'm waiting somewhere, or riding a bus or subway or whatever. I choose a person and try to imagine how I could dress them. I try to guess what their personality is like, and then I choose the kind of clothes I think they would look best in, depending on their body shape and coloring and all that. It's kind of weird, I know, but it helps pass the time.

At the stop just before mine I saw a guy who looked just like Joey. For a minute I thought it was him, and I was about to call to him when I realized that it wasn't. Just wishful thinking, I guess.

When I got off the subway in Chinatown, I started walking, hardly knowing where I was going. I made my way through streets crowded with throngs of shoppers and street vendors. Peddlers lined the sidewalks, selling electronics, toys, and clothes. Chinese women stood in front of the produce stands, haggling over the price of vegetables and fish. As I walked I realized that this was going to be more difficult than I thought. I had heard Ben mention the Orient Grill, but I had no idea where it was. I thought about asking someone, but I saw no one I wanted to ask. Everyone was intent on their own business, hurrying to get wherever they were going.

Finally I saw the Red Dragon, where Suni said Brad Hsu worked. I stood on the curb outside it and looked in. There was a HELP WANTED sign in the window and a menu offering the usual Chinese fare. I went in, hoping to find Brad.

The restaurant was open, but it was dark and quiet. It was too early for dinner and too late for lunch. Two old men sat at the bar, one drinking Chinese tea, the other drinking beer.

A boy was filling saltshakers at a table near the bar. I went over to him and asked if he knew Brad. "Sure," he said. "He's in the back. I'll get him."

He disappeared and was back in a moment with Brad. Brad looked surprised to see me, but he did recognize me. He said, "Hi. You're Suni's friend, aren't you?"

I nodded. "An-ying Chang. You were in my biology class last year."

"Yeah, I remember. So what are you doing down here? Don't tell me you want a job. I'm just a busboy, and believe me, there's got to be a better way to make some money, right, Danny?" he said to the other boy.

"Got to be," said Danny as he wiped down a table.

"No, that's not why I came," I said.

"No?" He looked puzzled.

I pulled out a picture of Ben. "I'm looking for my brother, Ben. I know he hangs out in Chinatown a lot, and I thought you might have seen him."

Brad took the picture of Ben and studied it. He glanced at me, and then back at the picture. Finally he said, "Yeah. I think I've seen him around."

"Do you know where he might be? He's been missing for two days. I've got to find him."

"I haven't seen him in a while." He began wiping the table, not really thinking about what he was doing.

"I've heard him talk about a place called the Orient Grill. Do you know where it is?"

"It's down on Pell Street, but if I were you, I'd stay away from there."

"Why?" I asked.

"I just would. Take my word for it."

"Look, I have to find my brother. I know he hangs out there, so it's the logical place to look for him."

Brad hesitated. Finally he said, "The Green Dragons hang out there. I wouldn't go down there asking questions—they don't like people who ask questions. If your brother's involved with the Green Dragons, well, I'd stay out of it."

The Green Dragons. A Chinese gang that operated in Chinatown. They were into drugs and selling counterfeit merchandise. I'd heard of them because my uncle and my father were always complaining about the gang violence and all the problems they were causing the merchants in Chinatown. I didn't want to believe Ben was involved with them, but it would explain a lot of things, like the phone calls and the money.

"Pell Street. That's two streets over, right?"

"Yeah, but . . ."

"Thanks. See you at school."

I left before he could say any more. I knew he was just going to tell me not to go down there again, and I didn't want to hear it. I walked the two blocks to Pell Street and turned right, looking for the Orient Grill. After a few minutes I saw it. I stood across the street from it, wondering if I should take Brad's advice. Finally I crossed the street and went in. The walls were lined with video games, and the place was packed with boys. A lot of them looked even younger than Lee. A lot of older guys were there too, most of them sitting at the counter or in the booths in the back. I saw only one or two other women, and I felt really out of place. I looked around for Ben, but I didn't see him.

I was wondering if I should ask someone about him when I saw one of the guys who had been at our house the night Ben disappeared. It was the short fat one with his head half shaved. He glanced in my direction and then stared at me, and I wondered if he recognized me. He had only seen me for a minute the other night, but the way he was staring at me scared me, and I decided to get out of there fast.

As soon as I was outside I began to run. I wanted to get as far away from there as I could. I ran until I came to the entrance to the subway, where I finally stopped. I stood on the corner, panting, trying to catch my breath and watching as the light faded and the streetlights came on. A cold wind seemed to cut right through me, and I started to shiver. I didn't know where to go or who else I could talk to, and I knew it would soon be dark. I decided there was nothing more I could do that day. I went down into the subway, praying that when I got home, Ben would be there, but knowing somehow that he wouldn't.

I got home just in time for dinner. Ben hadn't come home, and my parents were more worried than ever. I could tell that my mother had been crying again. She didn't question me about where I had been. I guess she thought I really had been studying for my history test.

I did have a test the next morning, and not only had I not studied, I hadn't even done all the reading. I hurried through dinner and then went right up to my room, but when I tried to concentrate on my books, my mind wandered, and I found myself thinking about Ben.

I don't know how much time had passed when the phone rang and Ma called that it was for me. I figured it was probably Suni, because she was studying for the history test too, but when I came to the phone, Ma was frowning. "It's that boy from school again," she said. I took the phone and when I heard Joey's voice, my heart started pounding. I was glad he had called, but I didn't really want to talk to him right then. There was too much else going on in my head. My mother was right around the corner, and I didn't want her to hear, so I took the phone and went into the hall closet, where I always go when I want privacy on the phone.

"How are you?" he asked.

"Okay. I've got a killer history test tomorrow. I'm trying to study, but it's not going very well."

"I'm calling from work, so I can't talk too long either. I just wanted to know if we can still get together. Is Friday night okay?"

"Um—I'm not sure right now. Can I let you know?"

"Waiting to see if something better comes along, huh?" He said it jokingly, but I could tell he was hurt. I didn't want to hurt him, but it was all so complicated. I couldn't even think past tomorrow. "No. It's not that, I promise. I really want to see you. I . . . I've been thinking about you a lot. It's just that things around here aren't too good right now."

"What do you mean?"

"Well, my parents are kind of . . . old-fashioned. Actually, they're prehistoric. They don't think I should date. Especially guys who aren't Chinese."

"Hmmm. I could disguise myself. Plastic surgery is an option."

I laughed. "Maybe it would be easier if we just met somewhere."

"Great. Where and when?"

I hesitated again. It was just so hard to think. I still wanted to look for Ben, and I knew I wouldn't be able to have any fun until I knew where he was.

"An-ying?" said Joey when I didn't answer.

"I'm just thinking. See, my parents aren't the only problem. It's my brother. He—he's missing, and it's my fault, and I have to find him." I hadn't meant to tell him, but before I knew it, the whole story came out in a rush. I was crying on the phone as I told Joey all about how I'd been to Chinatown to look for Ben and about the two guys who had come over Monday night. "I don't know what to do," I said. "All I know is I have to find him. I'm going back to Chinatown to look for him tomorrow."

"Listen. I have a friend here who lives in Chinatown. He knows a lot of people down there. Maybe he can help. I'll meet you there tomorrow and we'll talk to him."

"Really? Don't you have to work?"

"I get off at three, and I don't have to be at the recording studio until eight. I'll meet you at the N train at Canal Street. How about four-thirty?"

"Okay."

"I have to run. Don't worry—if anyone can find him, Dennis can. I'll see you tomorrow."

When I hung up, I felt much better. Just knowing I would be seeing Joey tomorrow made me feel good. I went back to my books, but I still couldn't concentrate. Now I couldn't keep my mind off Joey. I finally decided just to go to sleep and not worry anymore.

That night I dreamed that I went back to the Orient Grill, and this time Ben was there. I kept trying to talk to him, but he wouldn't answer. He acted as if he didn't know who I was, as if he'd never seen me before. At one end of the room there was this door. At first it was shut, but then it opened and the guy with half his head shaved came to the opening and called Ben. Ben got up and followed the guy into this long, dark tunnel. I kept screaming for Ben not to go with him, but he couldn't hear me. In the dream I was sure that if Ben went with him, I'd never see him again. When I woke up, I was so scared I was shaking, and I couldn't get rid of the feeling that Ben was in real trouble.

7

As I left the house the next morning I told my mother I would be late coming home again.

"You are neglecting your sewing, An-ying," she said. "Look at how it's piling up. When do you plan to get to it?"

"I'll get to it this weekend. Right now I've got too much schoolwork. Suni and I are going to the library to study."

"Maybe if you spent less time talking on the phone, you would have more time for your work."

I knew she would make some comment about my phone calls. "I was studying for the history test," I told her. "We go over the material on the phone."

"Make sure you're home before dark."

I rushed out before she could say anything more. I knew I wouldn't be home before dark, but I didn't care. I was going to be with Joey, and that was all I could think about. Even the fact that Ben was missing didn't seem so bad.

All day I looked forward to seeing Joey. When I finally found myself in history with the test paper in front of me, I realized how unprepared I was. I tried to concentrate, to remember our class discussions with Mrs. Wesler, but my mind was a blank. The harder I tried, the worse it got. I couldn't write, I couldn't think.

There was a clock over the bulletin board at the front of the room. I could hear it ticking, and the ticks seemed to get louder and louder, but I still couldn't think of anything to write. The questions on the test paper in front of me didn't make sense. Why hadn't I studied? I was so angry. Angry at myself, and at Ben for distracting me. So many feelings were swirling around inside my head. The clock kept ticking, louder and louder and louder. I threw down my pencil, and before I knew what I was doing I was up and running from the room, leaving my blank test paper on the desk.

I ran down the hall to the girls' bathroom, tears streaming down my face. I would flunk the test. I hadn't written one word. But why should I care? My father wasn't going to let me accept the scholarship to Wharton anyway. I was fooling myself to think that he would. Everything seemed hopeless all of a sudden. I heard Ben's voice in my ears: "You work too hard, little sister." And then I was sobbing. "Ben, where are you? Why are you doing this to us?"

I leaned against the sink, my hands over my face. I heard the door open, and I knew that someone had come in. Then I felt someone touching my shoulder.

"An-ying?" said a gentle voice. I took away my hands, and in the mirror I saw Ms. Brady. She looked almost as upset as I was. "What is it? Can I help?" she asked.

I took a deep breath and tried to calm myself. Then I ran water and began to wash my face. I was embarrassed that Ms. Brady had seen me so upset. "I'm sorry. I . . . I just . . ." How could I explain it all?

She patted my shoulder. "Do you want to tell me about it?" she asked. I told her about the history test and how I hadn't been able to concentrate.

"It's okay. It happens to lots of seniors. There's a lot of pressure on you kids."

I nodded.

Ms. Brady handed me some paper towels and went on talking. "It's not only the pressure of tests and papers and college applications. It's also the fear of what's coming next, after graduation. It's scary. Everyone feels overwhelmed sometimes."

"But the test. I couldn't even think. I didn't write one single word."

"An-ying, I've seen your grades. As your adviser I know that you haven't gotten below a ninety on any test or paper all semester. Mrs. Wesler's not going to let one bad day ruin a record like that. I'm sure she'll let you take the test again in a few days, when you're feeling better. I'll talk to her myself, if you'd like."

I dried my face and hands and blew my nose. I took another deep breath and nodded. Ms. Brady watched me with a look on her face that was so full of sympathy and concern, I almost broke down again.

"So you don't need to worry about the test. But tell me what else is wrong. I can see that something is bothering you. Why don't we go to my office?"

As we walked down the hall to her office I thought about how much I should tell her. I wanted to tell her everything about Ben and Joey and my parents, although I'd been taught never to tell strangers our family business. But Ms. Brady's not a stranger, I thought. She's my adviser. My friend. She wants me to go to Wharton. Then in the back of my mind I could hear my father. "This is a family matter. Ours alone. It is no one else's business."

I decided I had to talk to someone. I wouldn't tell her about Ben, but I would tell her about some of the problems with my parents. When we got to her office, she moved a pile of papers off a chair near her desk and told me to sit down.

I hesitated, wondering where to start. I began to tell her about my parents. "They're both Chinese, of course. Very traditional. There's so much they don't understand. They think I should live like girls in China do . . . " I shook my head. "They just don't understand."

"That must be hard on you," she said.

I felt tears come to my eyes. "And the worst part is, my father doesn't want me to go away to college. He wants me to go to college here and live at home."

"But what about the scholarship? As I told you, I'm certain we can get you one. It's a great opportunity. You can't turn it down."

"He won't let me accept it." I shrugged. "What can I do?"

Ms. Brady's voice turned from gentle to firm. "He can't stand in the way of a chance like this. He has to let you accept it." She was quiet for a minute. "What if I talk to him? Maybe I can make him understand how important this is."

"He doesn't speak English," I told her.

"Well, how about your mother? Could I talk to her?"

I nodded. "You could try," I said, but I didn't have much hope.

"I'll call her tonight," she said. She handed me another tissue and said, "Now I've got to get back to these papers. Why don't you clean up and then go down to the nurse and rest until next period? I'll tell Mrs. Wesler where you are."

I stood up. "Thank you, Ms. Brady. You've been great."

"Well, you're one of my favorite students. Can't have you sniffling in the bathroom all alone, can we?"

I felt better after that and was able to get through the rest of the day. As soon as school was out I headed straight for the subway that would take me back to Chinatown. As I climbed up the stairs from the subway I saw Joey waiting right outside the entrance, and all I could think about was how good looking he was. When he saw me, he smiled. "Hi. You came," he said.

"Did you think I wouldn't?" I asked.

"I wasn't sure. I thought maybe your brother came back."

"He didn't, but I would have come anyway."

"I talked to Dennis. He's going to meet us at the China Moon. It's just down the street. This way," he said, and we started walking.

"Does Dennis live in Chinatown?" I asked.

"He's lived here all his life. That's why he knows so many people here."

"So he's Chinese?"

Joey nodded.

"How did you get to know him?"

"From Sound Waves. He works there too."

We crossed the street, and Joey pointed to a restaurant on the corner. "There it is," he said.

Inside, we sat down at one of the booths that lined both sides of the dining room. It was only about five o'clock, so the restaurant was pretty quiet. Joey looked at his watch. "Dennis said he'd meet me here right after work. He gets off at five, so he should be here soon. Are you hungry? I'm starved."

I realized that I had hardly eaten anything all day, and I was really hungry. But I didn't have much money with me, and I didn't want Joey to have to pay. The waiter brought us some menus, and I ordered a Coke.

Joey looked at me. "Aren't you going to have something to eat?"

"Well, maybe an egg roll," I said.

Joey studied the menu and then said, "We'll have two orders of egg rolls, two Cokes, the chicken lo mein, and an order of fried rice. And maybe some wonton soup." He smiled at me. "I told you I was hungry."

The waiter was back in a minute with our Cokes and egg rolls. When he left, Joey said, "So, tell me about your brother."

I sighed. "He's been missing for three days now. I'm really getting worried. My parents are going nuts."

"Have they called the police?"

"My father doesn't want the police to know. He would never call them."

"You think your brother's in Chinatown?" He finished one egg roll and started on the wonton soup.

I nodded. I told him about the Orient Grill, and what Brad Hsu said about the Green Dragons.

"So you think he's mixed up with those guys?"

"I hope not, but ever since he lost his job this fall, he's been hanging out down here a lot." I took a sip of my Coke. "And he always has money, even though he's not working."

"That's weird," Joey said. "I wonder if he is getting it here somehow."

"It's funny," I said. "When we first moved to New York from Hong Kong, back when I was ten, I used to love to come to Chinatown. It seemed like home. But now it seems, I don't know, foreign and sort of threatening."

"I still don't know my way around Chinatown too well," Joey said. "Maybe you can show me around sometime."

"Sure," I said. "I'd love to." Being with him, I thought, would make a big difference.

"My schedule's kind of crazy," he said, "but we can figure out a time."

"Is it hard having two jobs?" I asked.

He shrugged. "Sometimes. Like today I worked nine to three at the store, and then I go from eight to midnight at the studio. It's kind of a long day." Joey helped himself to the lo mein and offered the plate to me. "Have some. I can't eat all this. Anyway," he went on, "I need the money."

As I took some lo mein Joey looked up and said, "There's Dennis." He waved, and I saw a Chinese boy coming toward us across the restaurant. When he got to our booth, he gave Joey a high five. "So this is the famous An-ying?" he said as he slid into the booth next to Joey. "This guy hasn't been quite the same since he met you. At work I keep finding him staring off into space." He nodded. "Now I see what it is he's been thinking about."

I blushed, and Joey punched his shoulder. "Don't pay any attention to him," he said.

Dennis ordered a soda and fried rice, then leaned back in his seat, relaxing. "Oh, man, it's good to be out of there. What a day. After you left, it turned into a mob scene. You can't believe this one guy I helped just before I left. He's the reason I'm late. I couldn't get rid of him. He wants this CD, but he can't remember the name of the group or the name of the album. Just a minor problem, right? So I'm going, 'What kind of music do they play?' And he says, 'Oh, I don't know, kind of . . . like, folky, or country rock . . . but sort of new wave, you know?' And I'm going, 'Sure, buddy.' And this goes on for ten minutes. I'm going, 'Do you know the name of any songs they play? Any cuts from the album?' And he's like, 'Um, something about the night, or the moon, or moonlight.' Give me a break!"

Joey laughed and shook his head. "You wouldn't believe some of the weirdos we get in there."

Dennis rolled his eyes. "Some of them have the IQ of a tree."

"You shouldn't insult trees like that," Joey said.

The waiter brought Dennis's food, and after Dennis took a few bites he said to me, "So. Joey says you're looking for your brother."

"Yes. Here's his picture." I took Ben's graduation photo out of my wallet. "His hair's a little longer now, but he's pretty much the same."

Dennis took the photo and studied it. Then he nodded. "I've seen him around. But not for a few weeks. Can I keep this for a while?"

"Sure, if it will help."

He took out his wallet and slipped the photo inside. "I'll talk to some guys around here. Someone will know where he is."

"You really think so?" I asked.

"Yeah. Tell you what. I'll ask around tonight, and I'll meet you tomorrow after work. I don't get off till seven, same as you, right, Joey?"

Joey nodded. "I don't have to work at the recording studio tomorrow, luckily. Why don't you meet us at the Pelican, An-ying? It's a little place right around the corner from the store. Here's the address." Joey scribbled an address on a napkin and handed it to me. I took the napkin and looked at it. The Pelican was in Manhattan, but I could get there from Brooklyn by subway. It would mean making up more lies to tell my parents, but I had to do what I had to do.

Joey looked at his watch. "I better get moving. I've got to go home and change before I go to work." He signaled to the waiter for the bill.

Outside the restaurant Joey said to me, "I'll walk you to the subway stop. You going this way, Dennis?"

"No, man. I'm heading uptown. I'll see you later. I should have some news for you tomorrow, An-ying."

"Thanks, Dennis. I really appreciate this."

"No problem. Joey will make it up to me by taking all the difficult customers, right, bro?"

"Huh. I do that already."

"Yeah, sure." Dennis raised a hand and took a few steps backward. "All right, I'll see you tomorrow."

We waved and started toward the subway stop. "If anyone can find out where Ben is, Dennis can," Joey said.

We went down the steps to the subway and stopped when we came to the turnstile. "Well, I guess I'll see you tomorrow," I said. I didn't know how to express how grateful I felt.

He nodded. "Seven-fifteen at the Pelican." He put his hand on my cheek. "Don't worry."

"Okay."

He leaned toward me, and we kissed. It happened so naturally, without any awkwardness, and it felt so good. Finally I pulled away. "I better go. My parents will kill me as it is."

"Oh, yeah. The dinosaurs."

"Right."

He took a step backward. "Well, I'll see you tomorrow."

"Definitely." I went through the turnstile, and then turned back and called, "Thanks. For dinner, and for . . . everything."

He waved, and I ran to get on the subway before it left. I knew my parents would be mad, but I didn't know quite how mad. A couple of things had happened while I'd been gone that caused them to go ballistic. For one thing, it was almost seven-thirty by the time I got back. My mother was waiting for me in the hall by the door and started on me the minute I walked in. "So. You decided to come home finally."

"I'm sorry, Ma. I should have told you I'd be late, but I knew you wouldn't let me stay. I told you I had to study."

"And your friend Suni told me she didn't see you at the library. So where were you for the last three hours, I would like to know."

"You talked to Suni?" This was not good news. I had told Ma I was going to the library with Suni, but I had forgotten to tell Suni to cover for me.

"She called to talk to you at six-thirty. When I realized who it was, I asked where you were. She didn't know. So, now I know you've been lying to me."

"Ma, believe me, I wish I didn't have to lie, but you don't give me any other choice. If you'd treat me like a normal seventeen-year-old girl, I could tell you the truth, but you don't. You treat me like a child, so I have to lie. Anyway, I'm home. I'm fine. Everything is okay. So don't worry about it."

"Everything is not okay. First we find out you have been lying to us. Then your teacher calls. Your father is furious. I've never seen him so angry."

"My teacher? You mean Ms. Brady?"

"Yes. She seems to know more than we do about our daughter's plans. It seems she has your life all arranged for you. Don't you think you might have talked to us about this before going to a stranger?"

"Ma, I did talk to you. I told Dad I was going to apply for a scholarship to Wharton and that Ms. Brady's almost certain I can get it. And she's not a stranger, Ma!" I was shouting now. Their attitude made me so mad. Here was Ms. Brady trying to help me, and they act like she's butting into our lives.

"You don't have to tell people our business. Perhaps we don't want to take charity."

I put my head in my hands and groaned. I tried to

explain as calmly as I could. "It's a scholarship, Mother. It's not charity. It's something I've earned by working hard every day since fifth grade." I felt tears welling up and forced them down. "I've earned it and I'm going to accept it, no matter what you and Dad say. You can't take this from me!"

I ran upstairs to my room before I said anything more. I was so angry, I was shaking. I sat on my bed and tried to calm down. I told myself that they were just upset because of Ben. I knew how worried they both were. I knew that they had probably been worried about me too when I hadn't come home, but I couldn't tell them where I had been. Worst of all, I knew that tomorrow I'd be out late again, and I knew that once again I couldn't tell them the truth.

I had just started my homework when Melissa called. "What happened?" she asked. "Suni called me and said you were in big trouble. She's scared to call you because your mother is so mad."

I told Melissa all about what had happened today, even about Joey.

"So you really like him?" she said.

"I guess I do," I told her, and as I said it realized it was true. I did like him a lot. Maybe I was even starting to fall in love with him.

"This has been the most complicated day of my life," I said.

"Well, I guess it can't get much worse," Melissa said. "Try not to worry so much."

"Don't worry? That's what I just told my mother," I said with a laugh.

"Everything will work out, I'm sure," Melissa said before hanging up. "See you tomorrow."

As soon as I got off the phone my mother cornered me. "I just have one thing to say," she told me. "Your behavior is unacceptable. You're grounded for a week."

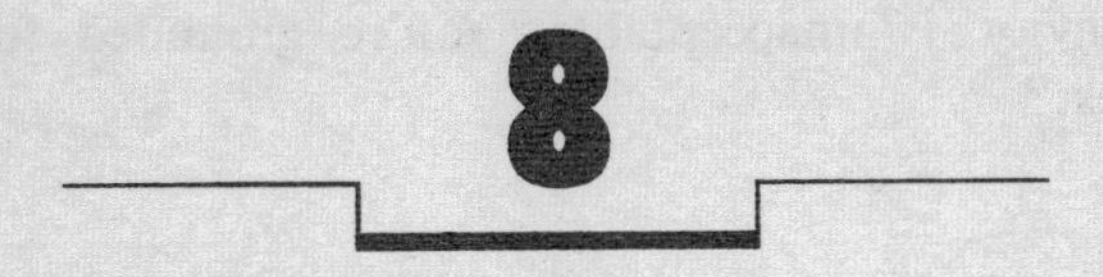

Suni, Melissa, and I met for lunch the next day in the cafeteria.

"I'm really sorry," Suni said. "I didn't mean to get you in trouble. The minute your mother said, 'She told me she was meeting you at the library,' I knew I'd blown it. I tried to make something up, but she didn't buy it."

"I know. It wasn't your fault. I forgot to tell you to cover for me." I unwrapped my sandwich and took a bite.

"She sounded really mad. Did she throw a fit when you got home?"

I nodded. "She grounded me."

"For how long?" Suni bit into her apple.

"A week."

"What are you going to do?" asked Melissa.

"I'm supposed to meet Joey and Dennis tonight at seven-fifteen at a place in the city called the Pelican. Dennis was going to try to find out something about Ben." I filled Suni in on what happened in the last two days.

Gary Lasiter walked by our table and grabbed one of Melissa's potato chips as he passed. "Hey," she called after him, but he kept on going. She sighed. "He's so good looking. Too bad he has the maturity of a two-year-old."

"So are you going to go?" Suni asked.

I nodded again. "I'll go home after school and tell my mother I'm going to eat early and then work in my room. Then I'll sneak out the back door while my parents are eating dinner."

"What if she comes to check on you or something?" asked Melissa.

I shrugged. "I've got to take the chance. By then she won't be able to stop me anyway."

"Yeah, but when you get home, watch out," Melissa said.

"I hope I'm home before she comes in to say good night. Just don't call me, whatever you do. If I get any phone calls, I'm dead."

"Are you going to tell Lee?" Suni said. "You could get him to answer the phone. That way if it's for you, he can cover."

"Good idea. I think I'll do that."

When the bell rang, I hadn't finished my lunch, but I felt better about my plan to sneak out. I might even get away with it, I thought as I loaded up my backpack and headed to math class.

At six o'clock that night I was ready to go. I fixed myself a quick dinner and told my mother I had tons of work and would be in my room all night. Then I went downstairs to talk to Lee. I knocked on the door to his room. "Yeah?" he called.

"It's me. Can I come in?"

"Yeah."

Lee was lying on his bed. His schoolbooks were spread out on the floor beside the bed, but he was reading a comic book.

"Oh, working hard, I see."

"Just taking a little break." He tossed the comic book aside and propped his head up on one hand. "What's up?"

"Look, I want to ask you something." I sat down on the end of the bed. "Will you do me a favor?"

"What kind of favor?"

"I'm going to sneak out tonight. They grounded me, but I have to meet someone. I told Ma I've got a lot of work and have to study all night. All you have to do is make sure to answer the phone in case it's for me. I just don't want Ma coming to look for me. Also, make sure the back door is unlocked so I can sneak back in."

Lee sat up. There was a pile of change on the bedside table. He picked up a quarter, tossed it into the air, and caught it. "Sneaking out, huh?"

I shrugged. "It's . . . important. I have to."

I guess he knew I wouldn't risk it unless there was a good reason, because he said, "Does this have something to do with Ben?"

I nodded. "I'm going to look for him. I'm so worried, and I feel like it's my fault he left."

"Your fault? Why?"

"Right before he left, we were talking, and I said something that made him mad. I really want to find him."

"You think he's okay?" I could tell by the way he said it that he was worried too.

"Yeah. I think he's okay, but I'd like to know for sure."

Lee nodded. "I'll answer the phone. And I'll check the back door."

"Thanks, Lee." I stood up. "I've got to get ready."

Lee picked up his comic book again. "You owe me," he said.

"Ha. Think of all the times I've covered for you."

"Seriously," he said as I reached the door. "Be careful. If Ma finds out, we'll both be in trouble."

"I'll tell her you didn't know anything about it."

"She'll never believe that."

"I'll be careful. Just make sure you beat her to the phone."

He nodded, and I went out and back upstairs to my room. I dressed in my best jeans, a blue chemise top that I made of scraps left over from a dress my mother had made for a customer, and a wool jacket I bought at a Goodwill sale. The jacket was originally a man's blazer and it was in pretty good shape, oversize like a lot of people are wearing them now. Anyway, when I looked in the mirror, I decided I liked the outfit. I brushed my hair, put on some lipstick and my silver hoop earrings, and then stood in the hall, listening.

I could hear my parents and Lee in the dining room, eating dinner. As long as they were in there they wouldn't see me sneaking out the back way. I crept down the hall, and as quietly as I could, eased open the door. I went out, holding my breath, and closed the door slowly and carefully, even though I wanted to slam it shut and run. I crept silently across the lawn. When I got to the sidewalk, I took a big breath of relief. Then I began to run.

At ten minutes past seven I stood outside the address Joey had scribbled on the napkin. A pink neon sign that said THE PELICAN told me this was the right place. In the window were advertisements for lots of different beers and a small sign that said, NO ONE UNDER TWENTY-ONE WILL BE ADMITTED. I stood outside, wondering if I should go in and see if Joey and Dennis were there yet or if I should wait. I didn't really want to walk in there alone, but what if they were already inside waiting for me? I was trying to see in the window when I heard Joey call me. I turned and saw him hurrying across the street with Dennis. Joey's hair was pulled back in its usual ponytail, and he was wearing a dark blue corduroy shirt and black jeans.

He looked incredibly handsome. In a minute he and Dennis were beside me, and the three of us went inside.

We sat down at a table in the back. I wondered if they would ask me for proof of age. If they did and we had to leave, I thought I would die of embarrassment. When the waitress came over to take our order, I was so nervous that I could hardly speak. We all ordered sodas. Luckily she didn't proof me. I was so relieved. I decided I must look older than I think.

When the drinks came and the waitress left, Joey looked at Dennis. "Go ahead and tell her," he said.

"Tell me what? Did you find him?" I asked.

Dennis took out the picture of Ben and slid it across the table to me. "I talked to some people who know where he is, but . . ." Dennis stopped. He twirled his soda can, watching it as if it would tell him what to say. Then he took a long drink. Finally he looked up at me. "I think your brother's in trouble. Real bad trouble."

"What do you mean?" I asked. I didn't really want to hear what he was going to say, but I knew I had to listen.

Dennis took a deep breath and let it out slowly, making his cheeks puff out. "He was working for the Green Dragons, probably selling drugs. Somehow he got on their bad side. He owes them a lot of money, and most of the gang members have turned against him. Apparently he wants out and they know it, and they're not going to let him off. A couple of these guys, well, they play hardball." He took another drink of soda. "They don't kid around, An-ying. He's in real danger."

"But where is he? Is he okay? Why doesn't he come home?"

Dennis shook his head. "He can't. I told you, he's in danger. These guys will kill him if they get the chance. He can't come home because that's the first place they'll look. Besides, it might put your whole family in danger. He's in hiding, and that's where he's got to stay, at least for the time being."

"So he's okay? Right now he's okay?"

Dennis nodded. "He's okay."

Joey slid his hand over mine. "I have to see him," I said to Dennis. "Do you know where he is?"

Dennis said nothing.

"You know, don't you?"

"An-ying, you don't want to see him. Believe me, it's not safe, and he . . . he doesn't want to see anyone right now."

I looked at Joey. "I have to talk to him. I don't have to stay long."

Joey looked at Dennis. "Do you know where he is?"

"It's really not a good idea, An-ying," Dennis said. "It could be dangerous."

"I don't care. I have to see him."

Finally Dennis nodded. "Okay. If it's that important to you. But I don't like it."

We finished our drinks and left the bar. We took a subway down to Chinatown, where Dennis led us through a twisting maze of back streets and alleys. He turned down a narrow dead end and stopped before a shabby tenement building. "He's up there. There are some rooms in the attic. A friend of his is letting him stay there for a while."

Joey and I looked at each other. "You sure you want to go up?" he asked.

I nodded.

Dennis knocked on the door. There was a row of buzzers, but none of them seemed to work, so he knocked again. Finally he pounded, and eventually we heard steps coming from inside and then a woman's voice. "Yeah? Who is it?"

"It's Dennis Lin. I'm with Ben's sister. She wants to see him."

"Hold on."

"That's Felicia. She lives with Wing Harper, a friend of Ben's."

There was a series of clicks while she undid the locks. Finally the door opened and a tall, thin woman stood in the doorway. She wore black leggings and a baggy black sweater, and her short hair was dyed red. She looked at Dennis and shook her head. "He's not doin' too well. You sure you want to see him?"

"Is he sick?" I asked.

She shrugged. "He'll be all right. He's kind of strung out right now. Not making much sense."

"I want to see him," I said.

The woman stood back and pointed to the stairs behind her. "Up there. Two flights. It's the door on the right."

I looked at Joey. "Come with me?"

"Sure. If you want me to."

"I'll wait down here," Dennis said.

Joey and I went up the two flights and knocked on the door at the top. At first there was no answer, so I said, "Ben? Ben, it's me, An-ying. Are you in there?"

Joey banged on the door louder this time, and finally someone said, "Yeah? What?"

"It's An-ying. Can I come in?"

There was a noise, like someone falling down, then footsteps, and finally the door opened. Ben stood there, holding one arm as if he'd hurt it. He was wearing the same clothes I'd last seen him in four days ago, jeans and a faded denim work shirt. His hair hung limp and uncombed, and his skin was gray. He stared at me with red, unfocused eyes as if he were trying to figure out who I was.

"An-ying?" he said finally. "What're you doing here?"

He sounded bad, like he could hardly talk. He spoke really slowly and he slurred his words.

"I came to see if you were okay," I said. "We've been worried." He stood back to let us come in, and I took a few steps into the little room. "This is my friend, Joey," I said. I looked around the room. There was nothing in it but a cot with a sleeping bag, a black-and-white TV that was on with the sound turned down, and a wood carton that served as a table. On it was a half-empty bottle of whiskey, a dirty ashtray, and several vials of pills.

Ben went back over to the bed and lay down. He looked like he had aged about twenty years. All I could do was stare at him. Finally I said, "Ben, are you sick?"

He tried to rouse himself, sat up, and said, "No, no. I'm okay. Jus' tired of being in this hellhole."

I sat down on the edge of the bed. "How long do you have to stay here? What's going on?"

He shook his head. "It's too—I—I can't tell you." Ben looked at Joey, who was standing in the middle of the room. "Who're you?" Ben asked him, as if he had just noticed him.

"I'm a friend of An-ying's," Joey told him again. "Look, you two want to talk. I'll wait downstairs with Dennis." He looked at me. "Okay?"

I nodded. When he had gone, I said, "Ben, what happened? Why are you here?"

He sighed heavily. I never saw him look so bad. "It's a long story." He reached for the bottle of whiskey and took a drink. "Got into some trouble, and now some people are looking for me. If they find me—" He shrugged. "We're not talking Boy Scouts."

He took another drink and held the bottle out to me. "Want some?" He smiled. "No. Course not. My perfect little sister wouldn't want to drink this nasty old stuff. That's only for bad boys and girls, right?"

"Ben . . ."

"Sorry." He sighed again and lay down. "Look, there's nothing you can do. I know you mean well, but you probably shouldn't have come here. You better go."

I was crying then. He was such a mess.

He sat up on one elbow. "Hey. Why're you crying?

I'll be all right. I gotta wait it out a few more days till the coast clears, that's all. Don't you worry about me, little sister."

I wiped my eyes and said, "Okay. But if you need anything . . ."

He took my wrist and held it. "Listen, don't tell Ma and Dad where I am. Promise me."

"But Ben, maybe they can help."

Ben snorted. "No. They can't, believe me. Promise you won't tell them."

He was sitting up now and seemed alert for the first time. He was squeezing my wrist so hard it hurt.

"Okay, okay. I won't tell anyone."

"Good." He released my wrist and lay back down as if he had used up all his energy.

"When will you be home?" I asked.

"Don't know, An-ying. Just don't know."

"Well, I'll see you soon." I hugged him awkwardly, tears running down my face. He seemed about to fall asleep again, but when I reached the door, he mumbled, "Hey, how's that Walkman I gave you? Working good?"

"Yeah, Ben. It's great. Really great."

"Good," he said, and closed his eyes.

I went out and stood at the top of the steps for a minute, trying to get myself under control. I took a few deep breaths, wiped my face, and started down the two flights of stairs. Joey, Dennis, and Felicia were sitting in the kitchen, drinking coffee.

"So," Joey said when he saw me in the kitchen

doorway. Felicia gave me a sympathetic look. "I'm telling you—he'll be all right," she said.

I nodded, although I didn't really believe her, and I don't think she believed it either.

"Thanks . . . for hiding him, and everything."

"Yeah, well, he and Wing go back a long way. I've tried to get him to eat, but he doesn't seem much interested in food. Those creeps will give up in a few days. They'll find someone else to worry about. Then we'll get him sobered up and send him home."

Joey finished his coffee and looked at his watch. "We'd better roll."

We left the house and followed Dennis back through the maze of streets, until we finally came to the subway station.

"I'll see you tomorrow," Dennis said to Joey. "An-ying, I'll see you around. Come in the store sometime. Joey and me'll give you the grand tour."

"Okay. As a matter of fact, there is a tape I want. Of course, I can't remember the name of the group or the title of the album, but . . ."

"She's all yours, man," Dennis said, laughing.

"Seriously, Dennis," I said, "thanks a lot for your help."

"Anytime," he said as he walked off.

"Are you going back uptown?" I asked Joey.

"After I take you home."

"But it's nowhere near the recording studio. You don't have to do that."

"I know I don't have to, but I want to. Okay?"

"Okay," I said. We held hands and walked down the steps into the station. A bum sitting on the dirty platform somehow made me think of Ben, and for a minute I felt really down. A vendor selling little stuffed animals called to Joey, "Your lady looks sad, man. You better buy her one of these to cheer her up."

"Good idea," Joey said. He looked over the array of animals and picked up a funny little cat that was curled in a ball with its head on its paws. "How much?"

"For you, a bargain. Just six dollars."

"Some bargain," I said.

But before I could stop him, Joey pulled out his wallet and gave the man six dollars. He handed me the little cat, and I smiled in spite of myself. "He is cute," I said.

"He reminds me of you," said Joey. "The way he's all curled up around himself. And his expression. Very mysterious."

"How is that like me?"

"You don't always say what you're thinking. You're mysterious."

"I am?"

"Very." He put his arm around me. "And lucky for you, I happen to love mysteries."

It was almost ten o'clock when we reached my street. I prayed that my parents hadn't found out I was gone. When we were a few houses away from mine, I said, "I have to go in the back way. They don't know I'm out."

He kissed me, just one quick kiss. I was too nervous

to think about anything except what my parents would say if they caught me out here with him. "Good luck," he whispered. "I'll call you." Then he was gone, and I crept around the back of the house, praying that the back door was still open.

I turned the knob slowly and opened the door. I closed it carefully behind me, then went quickly down the hall to my room. Inside my room I leaned against the door, breathing a sigh of relief. Had it really worked, I wondered, or had my parents discovered that I was gone? Quickly I changed back into what I had worn to school that day and went out to the kitchen, as if I had just come out to take a break.

As I went into the kitchen I was surprised to hear voices coming from the living room. I stood listening, and realized that it was my aunt and uncle. They and my parents were talking about Ben. I went to the door of the living room and said, "Hi, everyone."

"There she is," said my aunt. "Your mother told me you had locked yourself in your room to study."

So they hadn't missed me. Relief swept over me. I nodded and said, "I have midterms coming up."

"I tell you, you work too hard. Come here and give your poor old aunt a kiss." Aunt Su-lin held out her arms, and I went and kissed her. "Would you be a dear and get us some more tea?" my aunt asked.

I took the cups and went to the kitchen to refill them, knowing that my aunt wanted me out of the room. From the kitchen I could hear them discussing what to do about Ben. My uncle said he was going to look for Ben tomorrow, and that he would find him.

That was exactly what Ben feared. If my parents started looking for him and asking questions about him, they might lead the gang members right to him. I had to stop my uncle from looking, but how?

The teapot whistled, and I filled the cups and put them on a tray to take them back out to the living room. I didn't know what to do. Maybe the only thing to do was to tell the truth. I listened by the kitchen door. I had almost decided to say nothing when I heard my uncle say, "So tomorrow I will search Chinatown from top to bottom. If he's there, we will find him."

"But you can't," I blurted before I knew what I was saying. As I stepped into the living room my parents and my aunt and uncle looked at me curiously.

"What do you know about this?" my father asked.

"I . . . I know that Ben is in hiding, that he doesn't want to be found yet. He's okay, but he can't come home right now."

"You have spoken to him?" my mother asked.

"Yes."

"When?"

"I can't tell you any more. Just don't look for him. Let him alone, and everything will be okay."

"Sit down, An-ying," ordered my father. "Now tell us everything you know about Ben. I want the truth. All of it."

The teacups were rattling on the tray from my shaking hands. I put the tray on the coffee table and sat down. "I can't tell you where he is," I said firmly. "I promised I wouldn't."

"An-ying," said my uncle. "We know that Ben is involved with a gang. I have contacts with these people because of the grocery store. All the merchants in Chinatown know about the gangs. You do not understand how these things work, and I'm not sure Ben does either. These people are dangerous. Ben might think he can hide from them, but believe me, he can't. If we can find him, we can help him. I have many connections in Chinatown. I can protect him, at least for a while. But if we don't find him before the gangs do, well . . ." My uncle shrugged.

"An-ying, if you know where he is, you must tell us," my aunt added. *"Yiding."* You must.

The four of them watched me. I looked at my mother's face. There were lines of worry carved into her cheeks and forehead. My father looked old too. Much older. In spite of their lack of understanding, I knew that they truly loved their children, all of us, me and Ben and Lee. I knew that they were desperate to find Ben and to help him. I was so confused. I had promised Ben I wouldn't tell, but now that I was there with my parents and my aunt and uncle, I knew that I had to tell them. Ben was in no condition to help himself.

"He's in Chinatown. In the attic of a tenement on Mott Street. It's Wing Harper's place. He's okay."

"Wing Harper," my uncle said. "Yes. I have heard of him."

"How do you know this?" asked my mother.

I thought quickly. I couldn't tell them I had been there to see him. "I have a friend at school who knows

Ben. He works in Chinatown. I asked him to look for Ben, and he did."

"You should have told us right away," my father said.

"My friend told me not to. He said Ben didn't want me to tell anyone."

"It's only a matter of time before these people find Ben," my uncle said. "That's why we have to find him first."

My uncle arranged to meet my parents the next morning in Chinatown so that he could take them to Ben.

I couldn't wait to get out of the room so I wouldn't have to look into my parents' eyes. I got up as they were planning where to meet and slipped out. But my aunt saw me leave and followed me. Putting a hand on my shoulder, she said, "You did the right thing, An-ying. You had to tell us, for your brother's sake."

Had I done the right thing? I wondered. I didn't know if I just helped him or betrayed him. But I was glad for my aunt's support.

Most Saturdays I sleep late, but the next morning I woke up early and couldn't get back to sleep. I went out to the living room and found Lee flopped on the couch, watching cartoons.

I shoved his feet out of the way and sat down. He threw a pillow at me, and I tossed it right back in his face. "Listen. Thanks for covering for me last night."

"Yeah. Like I said, you owe me."

"Are Ma and Dad here?" I asked.

"No. I'd still be asleep, but they woke me to tell me they were going out. Haven't they ever heard of leaving a note?" he asked.

"They're going to Chinatown to look for Ben," I told him.

He looked at me, suddenly serious. "Do they know where he is?"

I nodded, then picked up the newspaper and began to read. I didn't want to tell him the whole story. I figured I should let Ben tell him himself, if he wanted to. Lee was still so young.

I got myself a cup of coffee and went back to the paper. A few minutes later we heard a knock on the door. Lee got up to answer it, but something made me stop him. "Wait a minute. Let me see who it is before we open the door."

I went to the window and looked through a crack in the curtains. Outside were two Chinese guys. One was the fat one who was at the house the night Ben disappeared. I had never seen the other before, but I sure wasn't about to open the door to them. I signaled to Lee not to open it and to be quiet. Then I went and checked the locks on the back door and all the downstairs windows. I closed all the curtains to make sure they couldn't see us. I came back into the living room and sat down on the couch. Lee sat down beside me and whispered, "Who are they?"

"I'll tell you later," I whispered. We sat on the couch and waited.

They knocked again, louder this time. Lee and I sat perfectly still, hardly daring to breathe. Lee turned down the sound on the television. It was frightening, knowing they were right there, just outside our door. We heard them talking to each other, then rattling the door handle. Then one of them pounded on the door as if he were trying to break it down. "Come on, Chang. Let us in. We know you're in there. You know you can't hide from us forever." More pounding. Quiet for a minute, then more talking.

A few minutes passed, and I thought maybe they left until we heard them trying to get in the back door. I was glad I made sure it was locked.

"You checked it?" Lee asked.

I nodded.

I guess it was only about five or ten minutes, but it seemed like hours that they were there. Finally I heard one of them say, "Come on. Let's get out of here." We heard them pass by the side of the house, and we figured they were gone. I let out a big sigh of relief. I'd been so scared. Lee stood up and started toward the front window, when suddenly it exploded and a rock whizzed by, just missing his head. For a minute we were both too startled to move. It happened so fast, we weren't sure what it was. We just stood there, staring at the rock and the shattered glass on the rug. Then we looked at each other. Lee looked as scared as I felt. "Who are they?" he whispered.

"They're looking for Ben," I said.

I got up and went to the window in time to see them pulling away from the curb in a blue Ford. I tried to see the number on the license plate, but they were gone before I could get it.

"They're gone," I said, turning to Lee. I was shaking so bad, my legs felt like they were going to buckle under me.

"Those jerks. Why would they do this?" he asked. He picked up the rock and weighed it in his hand. "I wish they were still out there. I'd throw this at their heads."

"Hey. I'm just glad they're gone," I said. "Let's get this cleaned up."

We picked up the biggest pieces of glass and then vacuumed up the rest. Then we taped a piece of plastic over the broken window. "Wait till Ma and Dad see this," Lee said.

We had just finished cleaning up when the phone rang. I guess I was still pretty shaken up, because I jumped when I heard it. I grabbed the receiver. "Hello?"

"Hi. It's me. I just wanted to hear your voice."

Joey. When I heard *his* voice, I was so relieved. I sank onto the couch, feeling totally limp. "Oh, Joey, Hi. God, I'm so glad it's you. You won't believe what just happened."

"What? You don't sound like you."

The whole story came pouring out, and when I told him about the rock, he said, "I'm coming over."

"No. You don't have to. Really, we're okay."

"But I want to. I'll catch a bus and be there in half an hour." He hung up before I could say anything more.

"Who was that?" asked Lee.

"A friend."

"Who? Melissa? Suni?"

"No. A new friend. You don't know him. He's coming over."

"He?"

"Yes, he. And if you tell Ma and Dad, I'll cut out your tongue and feed it to the birds."

"I won't tell, but what if they come back while he's still here?"

"They won't," I said. "I'll make sure."

For a while I sat in my room, just staring at the wall instead of getting ready to see Joey. I think I was sort of in shock. Finally Lee called me. "There's someone at the door. Should I get it?" He was still as nervous as I was.

"It's probably Joey. Just a minute; let me check," I said. I quickly brushed my hair. Glancing down at my sloppy sweats and T-shirt, I decided I just didn't care what I looked like. Then I went to the front window and saw Joey waiting on the stoop. I unlocked the door and let him in.

"I got here as fast as I could," he said. "You okay?"

"We're all right now, but it was pretty scary." I pointed to the window where the rock had come in. "My parents will have a fit when they see that. Oh. This is my brother, Lee. Lee, this is Joey."

"Hi, Lee." Joey looked at the broken window and shook his head, frowning. "Jeez. Why would they do that? I mean, what's the point?"

"Who knows. Those guys are crazy." I sat down on the arm of the sofa. "They almost hit Lee in the head. Missed him by an inch."

Lee held up the rock they had thrown.

"Wow," Joey said. He took the rock from Lee and looked at it. "Lucky it missed you. This sucker could do some damage."

"Yeah, and he can't afford to lose any brains," I said. "He doesn't have many to begin with."

"Ha, very funny," my brother said. "At least I'm not a brainiac like some people I know."

"Hmm," Joey said. "Is your sister a brainiac?"

"Lee, why don't you go clean up your room or something?"

"Want some privacy, huh? What's it worth to you?"

"I'll lend you my Pearl Jam tape for a week."

"Deal. I'm going over to Fritz's house anyway. See you guys later."

Fritz, Lee's best friend, lived two blocks away. Lee grabbed his jacket and said, "The place is all yours. Use it wisely." And he was gone, slamming the front door behind him.

Now that we were alone, I was suddenly nervous. "You want something to drink?" I asked Joey.

"No thanks. I just had breakfast. Where are your parents?"

"They went to Chinatown to find Ben."

"Really? You told them?"

We sat on the couch, and I told him about what had happened last night when I came home.

"So they know where he is? What are they going to do?"

"Bring him home, I think." I looked at my watch. "I'm not sure when they'll be back."

"They won't be back for a while, will they? This is so nice. Just you and me." He moved over and put his arm around me. I thought about how he came all the way out from the city just to make sure I was okay. He really cares about me, I thought. Before I knew it we were kissing, lost in our own little world.

It was so nice, and for a few minutes I forgot

everything but the feeling of his lips on mine and our arms around each other. I'm not sure how long we had been there when I heard a car door slam out in the street. I jumped away from him. "I hope that's not my parents," I said, going to the window.

Luckily it wasn't, but I knew they might be back any minute. "Look, I wish we could stay here all day, but if they find us here alone . . ."

Joey groaned and stood up. "I know. I'm leaving. But I want to see you again soon. I'll try to call you tonight, okay?"

"Okay." He kissed me once more and then was gone. I stood watching from the window until he was out of sight.

After Joey left, I went to my room to read, but I couldn't concentrate. I knew that I should be worried and upset about Ben, that I should feel bad about lying to my parents and scared about the creeps who had come looking for him, but somehow, all I could think about was Joey. I sat on my bed, playing with the little cat he gave me, and I felt warm all over, as though no matter what happened, someone was there for me, someone who understood me, who didn't want me to be something I wasn't. Just knowing he was there made me feel like everything would be okay.

My parents came home about half an hour later, but Ben wasn't with them.

My mother noticed the broken window the minute she walked in the door. "What happened here?" she asked.

I told them everything, and showed them the rock.

"We shouldn't have left the kids here alone," she said to my father. "I knew it."

"We're okay, Ma. Lee's fine. He went over to Fritz's."

"I think we should call the police," said my mother.

My father sat on the couch, looking exhausted. My mother and I joined him. "We will not call the police," he said.

"Did you see Ben?" I asked.

My mother nodded.

"He is *ni,* a disgrace to this family, a disgrace to our ancestors," my father said. "I don't wish to discuss him." He got up and went into his bedroom and closed the door.

"What happened? Where is he?"

My mother just sat there with her face in her hands. Finally she said, "He is still in hiding. Your uncle will protect him for a few days. We are trying to find money to pay off all he owes. But it is so much money." She picked up a picture from the coffee table of Ben and me and Lee, taken about four years ago. Her eyes filled with tears as she looked at the photograph. "He was never a bad boy. How did this happen? When did it happen?" Tears were flowing down her cheeks, and she looked at me with a pleading expression, begging me for an answer.

I sighed. "I don't know, Ma. He didn't mean for it to happen. He just . . . made a mistake."

"Yes. He made a mistake. And now we must pay for his mistakes. We all must pay." She wiped her face and continued to stare at the picture. "We came to this country because we thought it would be best for you children. Land of opportunity, they told us." She sighed heavily and said, "Maybe we should never have come here."

"Don't say that, Ma. We have a good life here. It was hard at first, but it's working out."

She went on as if she hadn't heard me. "First Ben, and now you. Out running around till all hours, never home on time. . . ."

I could hardly believe what I was hearing. "How can you compare me to Ben?" I shouted. "I'm getting straight A's. I'm planning to go to college. I haven't done anything wrong. Just because Ben screwed up doesn't mean I will too. It's not fair to say that."

My mother said quietly, "Chinese girls do not shout at their mothers. Have you no *shou?* No respect for your mother?"

I was so angry, I felt like throwing something. I tried to control myself, but I was still shouting. "In America, people are allowed to express their feelings. You are not being fair to me."

She looked at me, her lips compressed into that thin straight line, her face a blank once again, hiding everything she felt. "Go to your room, An-ying," she said.

I got up from the sofa, grabbed my jacket, and left the house. I didn't know where I was going, but I couldn't stay in that house one more second. I went down the front walk and crossed the street. I didn't look back, but I knew my mother's face was in the window, watching me go.

10

I hadn't planned on going to Suni's when I left the house, but I found myself heading in that direction, so I decided I would stop by and see if she was home. Her house is about a twenty-minute walk from mine, and by the time I got there I had calmed down a little, but I was still really mad. It was all so unfair. How could my mother compare me to Ben? Why wouldn't they let me grow up, and become the person I wanted to be? I had changed, like everyone does when they grow up. And I had to change to make it in America.

At Suni's house I went around to the side door and knocked. A window on the second floor opened, and Suni's head popped out. "An-ying? I can't believe it! I was just thinking how I needed you right now, and here you are. You must have ESP or something. Hold on. I'll be right down." The window slammed shut, and in a minute Suni was unlocking the door.

Inside, the Tabors' kitchen was warm and familiar and smelled of the almond cookies that Suni's mother liked to bake. "Come on upstairs," Suni said, and as I followed her up to her room she went on, "This is so perfect. Guess what happened? Jason called and asked me to go to the movies with him. A real date, can you believe it?"

"Suni, that's great! It's about time he got the message."

"I know. I've had a crush on him for almost a year. And we had such a great time at Michael's party, but then when he didn't call all week, I couldn't figure out what was going on."

When we got to her room, she took my hand and pulled me over to her closet. "Now. You have to help me figure out what to wear. Thank God you're here. I'd never be able to do this alone."

Suni has the nicest room. She's an only child, and both her parents work. Her mother is a nurse and her father has a small construction company. When they moved to this house three years ago, Suni was allowed to fix up her room any way she wanted. She sponge-painted her walls in two shades of peach, which looks so good, and she found a great bedspread that has sort of an Aztec print that looks perfect with the walls. It's a cool room, and I always feel good when I'm there. She also has a big closet with lots of clothes.

"A movie, right?" I said. "So you don't want to be dressy. Let's see." I started looking through the clothes, pulling out some shirts and pants I liked. "I love this," I said, holding up a turquoise silk blouse. "What pants do you have to go with it?"

"I think that's too dressy," she said.

She tried on about fifty different outfits, and finally we came up with the perfect look: her new black jeans and a soft mohair sweater with a cowl neck.

"That sweater is a great color on you," I told her. It was sort of a purply violet and looked fantastic with her black hair and dark eyes.

"You're sure this is right?" she asked, hanging up the rejected clothes.

"Trust me. You'll look super," I told her. I sat on the bed, peeling the label off the bottle of Pepsi that Suni had given me.

"So, why'd you come over? Any special reason? I mean, besides the fact that you received my urgent telepathic message."

I told her about the fight with my mother, and how I stormed out of the house. I also told her about the guys who came looking for Ben, and the rock, and everything.

"I don't believe it," Suni said, standing in the middle of the room. "I'm really sorry I went babbling on about what to wear to a stupid movie when you've been through all this."

"That's okay. I was glad to get my mind off it. I'm still so mad at my mother, though."

"I don't blame you. I can't believe she told you to go to your room."

"I couldn't believe it either. I mean, I know she's

upset about Ben, but she doesn't have to take it out on me."

"What are you going to do?" Suni asked.

"I don't know. I can't go on lying to them all the time and sneaking out. I wish I could tell them about Joey, but they'd absolutely lose their minds. What do you think I should do?"

"I think you should stand up to them, An-ying. You should be allowed to live your own life. You're almost eighteen. And it's not like you're doing anything wrong. You just want to be treated like a normal teenager."

I sighed. "I only hope this thing with Ben doesn't make my parents even more paranoid than before."

"What are they going to do? Chain you to your bed?"

I laughed. "With my parents, it's a possibility."

It was late afternoon by the time I left Suni's. I was still angry at my mother, but I felt a lot better than I had that morning. Since I was still grounded and I didn't want to risk sneaking out again, I spent the rest of the weekend studying and catching up on sewing.

The following Monday afternoon I was in my room studying when the doorbell rang and I heard my parents greeting my aunt and uncle. I knew they had come to talk about Ben. I could tell from their somber voices that the news was not good. I wanted to hear what they were saying, so I went to the kitchen and pretended to be making tea. From there I could hear them.

"I'm afraid it's the only solution," my uncle said. "It's not possible for us to raise that much money. And if they are not paid, who knows what they will do? I know these people—they're fiends. They will stop at nothing."

"Isn't there anything else we can do?" my mother asked.

"Believe me, we've tried to think of everything, but there is nothing else to be done. It's the only way to protect him."

"It's the only solution," my father added.

I heard my mother begin to cry. "It's not forever, An-mei," my aunt said. "Hong Kong is not the moon."

"It might as well be," my mother said.

Hong Kong. They were sending Ben back to Hong Kong.

"Lin-tao and Hu-sun will take good care of him," my aunt went on. "They will straighten him out. It's best, An-mei."

The teakettle began to hiss, but I was too upset to notice. Ben would be gone. It might be years until I saw him again. My aunt heard the teakettle and came out to the kitchen. She found me in tears. "So you heard," she said.

I nodded.

My aunt sighed. "His life is in danger. If we don't get him out of here, and quickly, they will kill him."

"Does he want to go?" I asked her.

"He has no choice. At least there he will be safe."

"But where will he stay? What will he do?" I asked.

"He will stay with your aunt Lin-tao and uncle Hu-sun. It's all arranged. Hu-sun will help him find a job in Hong Kong."

"When is he leaving?" I asked.

"As soon as we can make the arrangements," she told me. "The sooner the better."

I started to cry again, and my aunt tried to comfort me.

"It may only be for a year or so," she said. "Just till he gets himself back on his feet."

My parents arranged for Ben to leave the following day. His plane was to leave from La Guardia Airport at seven P.M., and my uncle had agreed to bring him by our house first so he could say good-bye. I was in my room at my desk when Ben came to my door.

"An-ying?"

"Ben! Hi."

"Hi. I guess you heard, huh?"

He came in and sat on my bed as he had done so often before. I just nodded. I didn't trust my voice. He looked much better than he had the last time I saw him, and he seemed sober. When I thought that this would be the last time he would sit there talking to me, I felt tears come to my eyes, but I tried to hide them. I didn't want to make it any harder for him.

"Back to Hong Kong." He leaned on one elbow. "God, I can hardly remember what it was like."

"Neither can I," I said.

"You know, I never told you this, but after the first

few weeks here, when things began to go wrong, and Ma and Dad were always working, I started to miss it. I never really understood why we left."

"But . . . you always seemed so excited about America. You and Dad, you both were so sure it was the land of opportunity."

"I was just a kid then."

"Do you mind? Going back, I mean."

He shrugged. "What choice do I have?"

"If only you hadn't gotten laid off. If you'd had a job, none of this would have happened."

"If only. I've said that so many times in the last few days. If only I hadn't done this, if only I hadn't done that. It is what it is. And I've got a plane to catch."

I started to cry. I tried to hold back my tears, but I couldn't.

"Hey. It's not the end of the world. I'll be back." He smiled. "I'll wait till you get rich and famous and can support me, and then I'll come back."

I tried to smile, but I was crying too hard.

"Hey, look at it this way. No more fighting over the TV. You'll never have to watch the basketball championships again."

I managed a smile. "Oh, you're taking Lee with you?"

He laughed and stood up. "Write me," he said.

"I will." I threw my arms around him.

Out in the hall my uncle said, "Hurry up. The plane won't wait, you know."

I followed my brother out to the hall. Ben gave my mother a last hug. "Say good-bye to Dad for me." My father hadn't come out of his room. He wouldn't speak to Ben.

My mother nodded.

On his way out he gave Lee a high five. "Be good, kid. I'll write you." Lee ducked his head to hide his tears. Then Ben picked up his bags and followed my uncle out the door. Just before it shut, he looked at me and gave me a thumbs-up sign.

Then he was gone. My mother put her face in her hands and ran to the kitchen. Lee slumped down on the sofa and looked at the watch that Ben had given him. He wiped his eyes, trying to hide the fact that he was crying.

"Why did he give us that stuff? Didn't he know he was just getting himself into worse trouble?" Lee asked.

I sat down on the couch beside him. I didn't have an answer to his questions.

"Dad just doesn't care," Lee went on. "He didn't even say good-bye to Ben."

"It's not that he doesn't care . . . it's just that . . ." I sighed. "Well, he doesn't know how to show it, and he doesn't understand a lot of things."

"You think Ma will be okay? I've never seen her cry this much."

"Yeah. She'll be okay. Ma's pretty tough."

He nodded. "I'm going over to Fritz's," he said.

In the kitchen my mother sat on her stool at the counter. For once she wasn't chopping something or sewing. My father came out of his room and said, "So. They are gone?"

My mother nodded. "You should have said good-bye."

My father said nothing. He had been so angry at Ben lately. The two had hardly spoken in the last few months, but down deep I knew how much my father loved Ben.

"What good does it do not to say good-bye?" my mother asked.

I could see she was really mad. She usually wasn't so direct with him.

"It does no good," my father said. "You think I don't know that?"

"Then why didn't you?"

My father shook his head. "I couldn't," he said.

My mother picked up her vegetable knife and began slicing a ginger root. "Perhaps Ben understands."

11

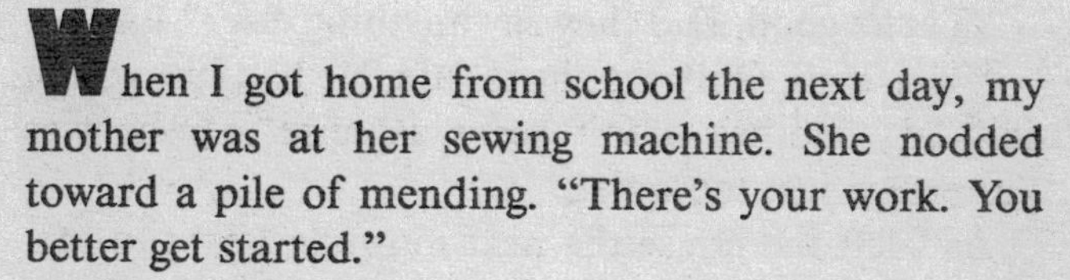

When I got home from school the next day, my mother was at her sewing machine. She nodded toward a pile of mending. "There's your work. You better get started."

My mother had been very quiet since Ben had left.

I was just about to sit down and start working when the phone rang. I grabbed it before my mother could get to it. Lucky I got it first, because it was Joey. When I heard his voice, I took the phone into the closet so we could talk in private.

I told him about Ben being sent away. "I guess it's for the best," I said. "At least he'll be safe there."

"It must be hard, though," he said.

"Yeah. I miss him."

We talked about school and about Joey's job. "Listen, my break's almost over, so I've got to go, but I've got the afternoon off tomorrow. Can I meet you after school?"

"That'd be great," I said. I wanted to see him badly, and I didn't think I could wait until the weekend.

"I'll be waiting for you outside at four o'clock."

"I'll tell my parents I'm going to the library. We won't have much time, but I really want to see you."

"Me too. See you tomorrow."

I hung up and came out of the closet, expecting my mother to attack me with questions about who it was, but to my surprise, she didn't even ask. I picked up my sewing and began to work.

"We heard from Hong Kong," she said. "Your brother arrived safely."

"That's good. Did they say anything else?" I asked.

"That's all. Only that he is safe. He had just gotten in." My mother didn't seem as upset as she was yesterday, just too quiet.

As I left the house the next morning I said to Ma, "I'm going to the library after school today, but I'll be home by six."

She nodded. "No later."

That would give Joey and me a couple of hours, anyway.

At school I got a chance to talk to Ms. Brady. I thanked her for calling my parents but told her it was better if she didn't do that anymore. I tried to explain about my father's pride, and how he worried about the family's reputation.

"Your parents should be proud of you," Ms. Brady said. "You're a strong person, An-ying. As long as you realize you're the one who is responsible for your own happiness, you'll do fine. I'm sure you will."

It felt good to hear that said about me, especially from someone like Ms. Brady. She always made me feel more like myself, somehow. I left her office smiling and feeling like I really could make things happen for myself.

At four, when I came out of school with Melissa, Joey was sitting on the lawn near the entrance to school, eating an apple. When I saw him my heart did its usual flip-flop. "There he is," I said to Melissa. I waved, and Joey stood up, tossing his apple core into a trash can. He stood there waiting for me, his hands shoved in his pockets.

"He's so cute," she whispered. "I didn't get a good look at him when I met him at Michael's."

"Hi," he said.

"Hi. Remember Melissa? You met at Michael's party."

"Hi, Melissa." He smiled.

I was nervous all of a sudden. It was strange, having him waiting for me here at school. It was like he was my real boyfriend. I could tell that he was nervous too. He rocked back and forth on his heels while we stood there.

"Well, I've got to get going," said Melissa. "I'll see you guys."

"Call me later," I said.

"Want to go get a soda or something?" Joey said.

"There's a deli right down the block. Let's go there," I said.

I ordered an ice tea at the deli, and Joey had a soda and a piece of pie.

"So how are the dinosaurs?" he asked.

"The same," I said with a laugh.

"Do they know about me?"

I shook my head. "You don't understand my parents," I said.

"You'll have to tell them sometime, won't you?" He leaned forward, elbow on the table, chin in his hand.

I poured a packet of sugar into my ice tea and stirred it with my straw. I sighed. "I don't know what I'm going to do. Suni thinks I should stand up to them. Stop lying and sneaking around and hiding, and make them understand that they have to let me grow up. But it's not that easy. Especially now."

"What do you mean?"

"Well, they're so upset about Ben."

"What do his problems have to do with it?"

"Just that they're so worried now," I said.

"What would they do if you told them you were going out with me?" he asked.

"They wouldn't let me," I said.

"How would they stop you?"

"It's hard to explain. Chinese families are . . . different."

"Yeah, I guess so." He reached across the table and took my hand. "I just want to be able to spend time with you," he said.

"I want that too," I told him.

We talked for a while longer, and then I noticed it was getting late. Joey said he'd walk me home.

When we got to my house, I knew I should tell him not to come up the walk with me, but I felt so stupid, always having to hide everything. He was only a year older than me, but he had his own apartment, and nobody told him what to do.

As we went up the walk I prayed that my mother wasn't watching.

"I have tomorrow night off," he said. "Can we do something?"

"Definitely." We agreed to meet after school Friday.

He kissed me and went down the steps. "I'll miss you," he said.

"Me too."

I went in and found my mother waiting in the hall near the door. I knew she had been watching us from the window. I didn't know how much she had seen.

"Who was that?" she demanded.

"Just a boy from school. I was studying with him." I dropped my backpack and went into the kitchen.

My mother followed me. "I don't want you walking around with strange boys. That is not acceptable. If your father saw this, he would . . . ha, you know what he would do."

I went to my room, slamming the door behind me. I knew it was worthless to argue with her.

Friday morning I told my mother I was going home with Melissa to study and have dinner. "Melissa's parents will bring me home later," I lied. I knew there was a chance my mother would call Melissa's mother to check up on me, but at this point I didn't care. I was going to see Joey, and that was all there was to it.

"You may go to Melissa's tonight, but tomorrow night your aunt is coming for dinner. I would like you to be here," she said.

When I got to math class, I told Melissa what I said to my mother. "According to my mother I'm going to your house to study, but actually Joey's meeting me here after school," I explained.

"Do you have any plans?" she asked.

"Not really."

"Want to do something all together? Alex has the car. Maybe Suni and Jason can come too."

Everyone liked the idea, so after school was out, I found Joey and we all piled into Alex's car.

We decided to go to a movie, and Alex headed for the Heights Cinema. It took us a while to decide on what to see, but we finally found something we all agreed on. The theater was crowded, so finding six seats together was impossible. Joey and I sat in two seats near the back, and soon after the movie started, he put his arm around me. Soon we were kissing. I have to admit, I don't remember much about that movie, but I'll never forget the intensity of the feelings I had for Joey that day. I couldn't believe it when the movie was over. I wished that we could have had some time to be alone together. Somehow I would have to find a way.

After the movie we piled back into Alex's car. "I'm starved. Let's get something to eat," Jason said.

Alex was just about to pull out of the theater

parking lot. "Okay. What'll it be? Left for hamburgers at the diner, right for Pizzatown."

"How about straight ahead for the Brooklyn Deli? It's right across the street," Melissa said.

"No way." Alex frowned. "Last time I ate there, I was sick for three days."

"You had the flu, silly," Melissa said.

"Maybe, but I still don't want to eat there."

"Well, what if everyone else does?" she asked.

"Everyone else isn't driving," Alex retorted.

"Pizza," Jason said.

"Hamburgers," Suni said.

"Pizza," Joey said.

"Pizza wins," Alex said. He took a right, and in a few minutes we were sitting in a booth at Pizzatown.

"Normally one large would do, but since Jason's here, we better get two," Alex said.

"At least," Suni said.

We sat talking long after we had finished the pizza, and I realized how well Joey fit in with my friends. Even though he was older and more experienced, he seemed to have fun with them and get along easily. I was so happy to be with him that I could hardly keep my hands off him, even as we ate our pizza. I kept squeezing his hand under the table, and we snuck a few kisses when we thought no one was watching. Finally we decided that we'd better get home, and Joey said he'd walk me there.

"I don't mind dropping you guys off," said Alex.

"Are you blind?" Melissa asked. "It's obvious they want to be alone."

Suni looked at me and winked. Then she said she'd call me tomorrow. Joey and I said good-bye to the others and started walking.

"I like your friends," he said when we were out of earshot. He put his arm around my shoulders and I wrapped mine around his waist, thinking what a perfect fit we were.

"They liked you too, I could tell. I'm lucky. I don't know what I'd do without my friends."

"Suni's Chinese too, isn't she?" he asked.

"Half. Her father's American. She was born in this country. Her parents are so different from mine." We were quiet for a minute.

"Sometimes I hate being Chinese," I said.

"Don't say that," he said.

"It's true."

"But being Chinese is part of who you are. It's not all that you are, but it's part of it."

"But it would be so much easier just to be a normal American teenager."

"What's a normal American teenager?" he asked. "It sounds very boring, if there is such a thing. We're all from another country anyway. I think it's interesting to be Chinese."

"First I was mysterious. Now I'm interesting?"

"Yes. Also beautiful," he said, leaning over and kissing me.

"Seriously, though, I'm thinking of changing my name. What do you think of Catherine? I'd like to be called Cathy."

"Why?"

"I don't like the name An-ying anymore. I'm not sure I ever really liked it. I just accepted it because my parents told me to. Like so many things. See, in China, girls aren't supposed to question anything their parents say. They're not supposed to think for themselves."

"But you think for yourself."

"I'm beginning to."

We had reached my house, and we stopped. He said, "If you want to be called Cathy, I'll call you Cathy, but I hope you change your mind. I love the name An-ying. And it fits you."

It was late, and I knew my parents were waiting for me. "I'll think about it," I said. "I better go in. My mother's probably called the police by now." I gave him a hug. "I really had fun. Thanks." I started up the steps, but he took my hand.

"Wait. What about tomorrow night? Can we do something?"

"I promised my mother I'd be home. My aunt's coming for dinner. But call me later. No, I'll call you so my parents don't get upset. I'll try to work something out."

My parents were watching television in the living room when I got home. I raced straight to my room before they could start lecturing me. A few minutes later there was a knock on my door. I thought it was probably Lee, but it was my mother. Uh-oh, I thought. Here it comes.

But to my surprise all she said was, "How are your studies going?" She hadn't been herself at all, and it upset me to see her looking so defeated and sad. Tonight, though, she seemed a little better.

"Okay. The chemistry exam will be the worst. Everything else should be pretty easy."

"I'm sure you will do well. You always do. Your aunt called tonight. She is very excited about our dinner tomorrow. She's bringing a special friend."

"A special friend? What do you mean, a special friend?" I asked. I couldn't believe she would try to set me up again. I had called her the day after the dinner with Paul Chun and explained that though Paul was very nice, I did not need her to arrange dates for me. I had tried to be tactful about it, but I was pretty sure I got through to her. My aunt has always been more understanding about stuff like that than my parents.

"You know your aunt. She's always got someone new she wants us to meet," said my mother.

It was true. My aunt loved meeting new people and arranging parties and dinners. She was always talking about someone we had to meet. I decided she was probably just trying to cheer up my mother and take her mind off Ben.

"I will need your help in the kitchen," she went on.

"I'll help you, but do I have to be here for the dinner? I was hoping to go out."

"Your aunt is expecting you to be here. I told her you would be."

I was disappointed, because I really wanted to see Joey again, but I could see that this was important to my mother. This was the first thing she'd seemed interested in so I decided to go along with her. Maybe I could see Joey on Sunday if he didn't have to work.

"Okay, Ma. I'll be here."

"Thank you, An-ying."

When she left, I went to call Joey. When he heard my voice, he said, "Is this An-ying or Cathy?"

"I don't know yet. I still haven't made up my mind. I'll decide by Sunday, which is the next time I can see you."

"Not tomorrow?"

"No. My aunt is coming for dinner, and I can't get out of it. Do you have to work on Sunday?"

"I do in the afternoon. The store's open from ten to four."

"How about if I come there and meet you? I'd like to see where you work."

"Great. Will your parents let you?"

I laughed. "Are you kidding? If I told them I was going into the city to meet an American guy at a music store, they'd have me locked up. I'll have to make up something, but that's okay. I'm getting pretty good at it."

"Are you ever going to tell them about me?" he asked.

"Soon," I said, but when we hung up, I wondered if I would ever be able to tell them the truth. My parents didn't seem to want to know me, who I really was. It was like they looked right through me, like I was invisible.

12

I slept in the next morning, and when I got up, my mother was already in the kitchen, cooking up a feast.

"Ma, you're making enough food for twenty people. What's going on?" I asked.

"I just want this dinner to be special," she said. "Your aunt and uncle have done so much for us."

I helped her chop vegetables and roll the dough, dip the shrimp in batter and mix sauces. Then I spent the rest of the afternoon studying, until it was time to get dressed. I had been planning to wear a new silk blouse I had made out of some leftover material and a pair of jeans, but when I went to change, my mother said, "Wear your good blue dress. You look so pretty in that."

"But Ma, that's so fancy. It's way too dressy for tonight."

"You know how your aunt is. She loves to wear her fine feathers. She'll be dressed up like a peacock."

It was true that my aunt did love to wear nice clothes, and if this was to be a special dinner, she probably would be all dressed up. Anyway, it was the first time my mother had seemed excited about anything since Ben had left, so I decided just to go along with her. I would feel kind of dumb in a fancy dress, but none of my friends would be there, so it didn't really matter.

After I took a shower and dressed, I went to help my mother set the table.

"Oh, you look wonderful," she said. She was dressed in one of her best dresses, and my father had on his good suit.

"Who is this guest?" I asked. "It must be someone pretty important."

"You'll see." My mother smiled. It was the first time I'd seen her smile in days. Well, I don't care who it is, I thought, it's good to see Ma happy about something. At least it gets her off my case.

It wasn't until my aunt and uncle arrived with this mystery guest that I began to understand. As soon as I opened the door and saw them, it hit me. There was my aunt, all dressed up, just as my mother had predicted, and my uncle, looking as uncomfortable as my father in a suit, and with them was a Chinese boy about my age.

"An-ying, you look lovely. Isn't she lovely, Son-li?" My aunt took my hand and said, "An-ying, this is our friend Son-li."

I couldn't believe it. When I saw the boy, I understood exactly what my aunt and my parents had in mind. I was so angry, I could hardly speak. I thought my aunt had learned her lesson after the episode with the photograph and poor Paul Chun, but here she was again trying to match me up with some dorky boy. When would they learn?

My parents and my aunt and uncle stood there smiling at me, waiting for me to say something to this boy. He was wearing a coat and tie and looked nervous and uncomfortable and . . . ridiculous. Why had this boy agreed to come? I wondered. Why hadn't he just said no?

The more I thought about it, the angrier I got. I jerked my hand away from my aunt and folded my arms across my chest.

"An-ying, say hello to Son-li," said my mother, as if I was some kind of puppet.

I said nothing.

"She is shy sometimes," my aunt mumbled to Son-li. She put her arm around his shoulders and practically shoved him in my direction. "Uh, hi, An-ying," he said.

"My name is not An-ying," I said. "It's Catherine. Call me Cathy."

There was a shocked silence, and they all went on staring at me. If I hadn't been so mad, I would have laughed at them.

"She's joking, of course," said my aunt. "An-ying has a wonderful sense of humor." She smiled at Son-li. "Why don't you two sit down and get acquainted?"

"I'm not joking, Aunt Su, and I don't want to get acquainted." Before anyone said anything more, I turned and went to the kitchen.

My aunt and my mother followed me. "An-ying, you are being rude. He is our guest," said my mother.

"I don't care if I'm being rude, and I don't care what he thinks. Why didn't you tell me what was going on? I know why. Because you knew I would never have agreed to this." I turned on my aunt. "I told you the last time you tried to set me up with someone that I don't want your help. I'm perfectly capable of making my own friends and deciding for myself who I will go out with."

"But An-ying," my aunt said, "in China, a girl's relatives arrange her marriage for her. That way they can all be assured that it will be a suitable marriage. We're not saying you have to marry this boy. We just want you to keep an open mind. He is very nice. And so handsome," she added.

"Marry him?" I was practically screaming, I was so angry. "Marry him? I don't even know him. How can you even talk about marrying him?"

"But in China—" my mother began.

"This is not China!" I screamed. "In case you haven't noticed, this is America. In America, parents wouldn't even think about trying to arrange a marriage. In America, parents respect their daughter's right to make her own choices, to live her own life."

"Shhh. Calm down, An-ying. He will hear you."

"I don't care if he hears me. I hope he does hear me."

There was no point in trying to explain how I felt to them. I turned and went to my room. I locked the door and lay down on my bed. I would not eat dinner with them.

First my mother, then my aunt, then my father came to my door and alternately begged and ordered me to come out, but I refused. It was the only way I could get through to them that I was serious.

For two straight hours I lay there. I could hear snatches of conversation from the dining room. I heard them tell the boy I had suddenly taken sick, but I'm sure he wasn't fooled. Soon after dinner was over, my aunt and uncle left, taking the boy with them. I heard my mother clearing the dishes while my father watched TV. I heard them talking and finally arguing, and then I heard something I had never heard before. My mother was actually standing up to my father. "No," I heard her say, "she is right. This is not China. Things are different here. We have to let her live her own life."

Was it possible that my mother was finally beginning to understand?

A few minutes later she came to my door, and this time I let her in. I got up, unlocked the door and opened it, and then went back to lie on my bed. My mother came and sat down beside me. I was surprised.

I had thought she would never forgive me for ruining her dinner and embarrassing her in front of my aunt and uncle.

"I'm not going to apologize, Ma," I said.

"Your aunt is very upset."

"I don't care. She should have known better than to try something like that."

"It was just a dinner. You're making too much of this."

"You know it was more than just a dinner. You and Aunt Su were trying to match me up with that creepy boy. You didn't even ask me about it first. It's like I don't even exist, like I'm invisible to you."

My mother sighed. "I've been thinking," she said. "All during dinner I was thinking. Trying to understand what had made you so upset. I still don't understand it entirely, but maybe you are right that we try to live too much like we are still in China. There is so much here in this country that we don't understand. So much that is different."

I was amazed to hear her say this. She was actually listening, for a change.

"You know," she went on, "a few days after we arrived in this country, I went to the grocery store with your aunt, and I saw a man and a woman pushing a grocery basket. They were having a disagreement about what kind of cereal to buy. The man had picked out a brand of cereal and the woman put it back and said, 'No. Not that kind. This kind is better.'

"'But I like this kind,' said the man.

"And the woman said, 'It's full of sugar and it's too

expensive.' The man shrugged and they kept the woman's cereal.

"I remember how shocked I was. First, that the woman would disagree with her husband in public like that, and then that he would give in to her so easily. And why, I thought, did the woman not let the man have the kind of cereal he wished? That is something you would never have seen in China. And I thought, What a strange country this is. I think that was the first time I realized just how different this country was. I still don't quite understand why she didn't let him have the cereal he wanted."

"But what about what she wanted?"

My mother shrugged. "A woman is happy when her husband is happy."

"Do you still believe that, Ma?"

She sighed. "I don't know anymore. It's not easy to unlearn things you've been taught all your life. I remember the day your father and I were introduced. The only thing I wanted in the whole world was to please him. I was so happy when he smiled at me."

I shook my head. "But you didn't even know him."

She shrugged again. "That didn't matter. He was the one my parents had chosen for me."

"I can't understand that."

"I know. I don't expect you to understand it. You live in a different world." She frowned. "I should never have listened to your aunt. She means well, but she doesn't understand. She has no daughters of her own."

I realized that this was my mother's way of apologizing for trying to set me up with the boy. She really was trying to understand me. And then I thought, Maybe I could try to understand her a little better too.

"It's hard for you living here, isn't it, Ma?"

"Your father and I will never fully adjust. We were too old, too set in our ways when we came here. But you, you can have everything this country can offer . . . education, a good job . . . a nice home for your family. That's the real reason we came. Not for us, but for you children. That's why we worry so much. We just don't want you to make any mistakes."

"I know that, Ma. But I have to be able to make my own decisions."

"About some things, yes."

"About who I plan to date."

"Yes." My mother nodded.

"As a matter of fact, I have met a boy, and . . . I like him. I don't mean I'm going to marry him, but . . ."

"But you like to be with him?"

"Yes."

"Is he Chinese?"

"No. Does that matter?"

My mother hesitated and then sighed. "I don't know."

"Sometimes I wish I weren't Chinese."

"Don't say that, An-ying."

"Why not? I mean it."

"And do you mean it about changing your name to Catherine?"

"I . . . I'm not sure."

She said nothing for a minute, and then she said, "You know, you are named for your great-grandmother, my grandmother An-ying."

I nodded.

"Yes. I named you for her because I knew when I was carrying you that you would be like her."

I smiled. My mother has very strange ideas sometimes. "Now how could you have known that, Ma?"

"Oh, you were always kicking and punching. You seemed even then to be telling me what you wanted. My grandmother was like that. She had a very strong personality. In fact, it was she who taught me how to be myself."

"What do you mean, Ma?"

"Well, it's a long story."

I laughed. My mother's stories were always long, but it had been a while since she had told me one, or maybe a while since I had listened. "That's okay," I said.

"Well," she began, "you see, when I was a very small child, I didn't want to be myself. I wanted to be my older sister, your aunt Lin-tao. Because it seemed to me that she was the one who got everything. She was the oldest, so she always got the new dresses, and I got her old castoffs. I thought this was very unfair. One day we were going to the festival, and once again, Lin-tao had a brand-new dress while I had her old tired one. I was so angry I refused to get dressed, and my mother told me that if I didn't get dressed, I would have to miss the festival, which, of course, I didn't want to do. Well, your great-grandmother An-ying came to me and she said, 'Why is it so important to you to have a new dress?'

"And I said, 'Because it would make me look nice.'

"'But you look nice in this dress,' she said.

"'But in a new dress I would look like somebody special,' I said.

"'And why is it important to look like somebody special?'

"And I said, 'Because then I would *be* somebody special.'

"'So you think if you look like somebody special, you will be somebody special?' she asked. And I nodded.

"'So if you put on a mask to look just like a cat, you would be a cat?'

"I said, 'No, I would just look like a cat.'

"And she said, 'That's right. You can never be anybody but who you are. You can look like somebody else, but you can never be anybody else.'

"And I said, 'But I don't know who I am. I am nobody.'

"'Well, I will tell you who you are,' Grandma said. 'Inside you there are little parts of thousands of ancestors. And then there is also everything that has ever happened to you all your life. Every tiny action, every little thought, it is all there inside you. So you see, that is a lot to have right there inside your small body. It's amazing that it all fits in so well, isn't it?

And there is still room for all that is to come. So when you say you are nobody, I laugh. How can you be nobody when you have all that inside you?' "

"So did you go to the festival?" I asked.

"Yes. And I wore the old castoff dress. And I still thought it was unfair that Lin-tao got all the new things. But I never again thought I was nobody."

She paused and then said, "So, I suppose if you want to change your name, I cannot stop you. But remember, changing your name will not change who you are. You live in America, but you were born Chinese. Nothing will change that. Perhaps rather than trying to change it, you should accept it and be proud of it."

"It's funny. Joey said pretty much the same thing."

"Joey?"

"The boy I was telling you about."

"Hmmm. I would like to meet this boy. He sounds very smart."

For my mother to say this was a big deal. In the past she would never have considered meeting him and would have forbidden me to see him again. It seemed that since Ben had gone, she had been doing a lot of thinking. "Actually, I think you'd like him, Ma."

"Perhaps," said my mother.

She put her hand up to my cheek, and I gave her a hug. It had been a long time since I had hugged her, and it felt good.

She stood up to leave, and I said, "Ma, I am going to accept the scholarship to Wharton if I get it."

"Well, we'll see what your father says about that."

"I don't care what he says. I'm going to accept it."

"Your father might not agree to that," she said. "He doesn't like the idea of your living with *waigoren.*" To my parents, all Caucasians were *waigoren,* or foreigners.

"What about you, Ma? What do you think?" The mask slid back over her face, and once again she wore the blank, unreadable expression that I had learned to dread.

"I cannot go against his wishes, An-ying."

"But Ma, do you know how much this means to me? How much it means to my future?"

"Your father will make the right decision."

"But . . ."

"Good night, An-ying."

When she left, I thought about all the things she had said. There was a lot I still didn't understand about my mother. And a lot she didn't understand about me. But I was beginning to understand myself a little better.

13

A little less than two weeks later I sat at the dinner table with my parents and Lee. I was waiting for Lee to finish eating and go to his room so I could talk to my parents alone. That morning Ms. Brady called me into her office and told me that I definitely won the scholarship to Wharton. "It's such a wonderful opportunity. I'm so happy for you," she said, giving me a hug.

All afternoon I walked around in a daze, picturing myself as I would be next year, a college student, on my own, free to come and go as I pleased, to be the person I want to be. But in order for that dream to come true, there was still one more thing I had to do. As I sat at the table that night, I was ready.

Lee was giving my parents a blow-by-blow description of a basketball game he'd played that afternoon. I wished he would just gobble down his food and ask for seconds like he usually did, but he seemed to be in one of his talkative moods. Well, maybe he would get my parents in good moods too, I thought.

Finally he finished and asked to be excused to go start his homework. When he was gone, I said, "Ma, Dad, there's something we need to talk about."

"What is it, An-ying?" asked my father.

"It's about next year," I said. "I heard from Ms. Brady today that I got the scholarship to Wharton. I told her I would accept it."

My mother looked at me and then at my father. He pushed away his plate and leaned back in his chair. "Why did you tell her that? I told you you're to go to school here in New York. I will not have you living in some dormitory with a bunch of *low faan.* It is out of the question. Call her now and tell her you will not accept it."

"I've already told her I'm accepting it, and I won't change my mind."

My father looked at me as if he couldn't believe his ears. "If you don't call her, I will. And while I'm at it, I'll tell her to stop interfering in my daughter's life."

"How are you going to call her, Dad? You don't even speak English," I said.

"Your mother will call her." My father spoke quietly, but I knew he was seething. He looked across the table at my mother. She was looking down at her plate.

"An-mei. If An-ying will not call this woman, you will do it. Tell her we do not want her charity."

"It's not charity, Dad. I won it by hard work. I have every right to accept it, and I'm going to accept it."

"An-mei." My father said my mother's name as if it were a warning. He sat perfectly still, his clenched fists resting on the table in front of him. His dark eyes shone with anger as he waited for my mother to say something. She looked at me and then at him. Slowly she shook her head.

My father pounded his fists once and leaned forward toward my mother. "An-mei. You will call this woman. You want your daughter living with barbarians? Have you heard what goes on in these dormitories?"

"Our daughter is almost a woman. We have to let her make her own choices. If this is what she wants, I think we should accept it." I could see my mother's hand shake slightly as she folded her napkin. Then she said quietly, "We have to trust her."

For a minute my parents stared at each other across the table. I couldn't believe my mother had actually said no to him. My father couldn't believe it either, and he looked at her as if he had never seen her before. The minute seemed to stretch into an hour. No one moved, or even seemed to breathe. My mother's face was flushed, her jaw tight. Finally my father stood up, pushing back his chair so hard that it hit the wall behind him. He stomped out of the dining room, and in a minute we heard the door of their bedroom slam shut.

My mother got up and began clearing the table, her face composed once again behind its unreadable mask. I knew what it cost her to defy my father like that, and I wondered if he would ever forgive her.

"Thank you, Ma," I said, fighting back tears. I put my arms around her and hugged her.

She hugged me back for a minute, and then said, "I don't want to lose you, too."

I think she finally realized that she could lose me, just as she lost Ben, if she didn't make some changes.

"Help me clear now, An-ying. I have to get your father his tea and biscuits."

She went into the kitchen, and I began to gather up the rest of the dinner things. I thought about what my great-grandmother An-ying once said, how we are made up of bits of all our ancestors, plus everything that has ever happened to us, with room for all there is to come. I knew there was a lot to come, but I also knew that something really big already happened, and it had changed me forever.

I hurried into the kitchen with my arms full of dirty plates and silverware. I planned to call Joey just as soon as the dishes were done.